AGENT

'The best of Thomas Hinde's novels have always been constructed on two levels. Upstairs his characters go about their worldly business; but each move that they make sets up metaphysical and ethical reverberations in the labyrinthine cellars below them. His latest book, *Agent,* follows this pattern.

'On one level it is a thriller about an English agent who, parachuted into a foreign country, finds himself terrifyingly isolated from the other agents whom he is supposed to meet and from his bosses back home. On another level it is a book about the inability of one human being ever to rely totally on the loyalty of another.'

Sunday Telegraph

Agent

Thomas Hinde

CORONET BOOKS
Hodder and Stoughton

For Cordelia

Copyright © 1974 by Thomas Hinde

First published 1974 by Hodder and Stoughton Ltd

Coronet edition 1975

Printed and bound in Great Britain for Coronet Books, Hodder and Stoughton, St. Paul's House, Warwick Lane, London, EC4P 4AH By Cox & Wyman Ltd, London, Reading and Fakenham

ISBN 0 340 20140 1

Part One

LENA is coming tonight.

She does mimes for me. Right in the middle of one she'll burst into tears, though she won't show it. She'll keep her face turned away from me, trying to hide them, continuing her act, but I'll catch glimpses of her crumpled face and see flashes of light reflected in the drops on it. Things have happened to Lena which should never have happened to a girl of her age — what a mistaken thought. It's because of what's happened to her that I so admire her.

One of her silent mimes is a Visiting Trooper. She throws out her chest, struts, kicks up her knees, stares at a far corner of the ceiling. The look on her face of idiot pride makes me laugh aloud. Suddenly, however anxious I've been all day, her expression, or two in quick succession so that I don't have time to recover between, jerks a chuckle from me. Once that's happened I can't stop.

5

Perhaps I'd find her less funny if she ever explained what she was miming, but she never does.

There's one in particular I don't understand, though I believe it's a Visiting Officer. She grips a rolled newspaper under her arm, perhaps representing a swagger cane. Presently she uses the point to lift something, holds it up in amazement, draws it close to her eyes, even curves her arm behind her shoulder, as if trying to peer at its far side. This Visiting Officer has found something he's too stupid to understand, though everyone else can.

Usually she does her mimes naked. There seems a connection: they start the moment her clothes come off.

Afterwards we make love like animals. Young happy animals.

Lena works in the canteen. Carefully I began to ask about her, but never more than once of a particular person, so that he'd guess my interest was more than casual.

'Poor old Lena,' I was told — she isn't old. 'Twenty,' she once told me with such exaggerated despair I shook with laughter — and guessed that this was what she'd hoped for.

She was, I gathered, slightly deranged, as a result of losing both parents at once when she was in her mid-teens. Luckily she was capable of canteen work provided the workers didn't mind occasionally getting reconstituted mash and beans when they'd asked for the grease-smeared slices of fortified white pulp they call bread and butter here.

Perhaps for a time she *had* been deranged and had discovered that this put her into a relationship with other people which she preferred. Perhaps she'd half-intentionally retained her oddities: her habit of holding her nose close to the food she's about to hand you, for example, sniffing and curling it in disgust, or of making remarks like 'looks red' as I once heard her when someone said it was a fine day, or of simply staring at you when you ask whether she's put any sweetening in your instant coffee substitute, so you wonder what on earth you've said. Lena's no more mad than they are — a lot less.

Sometimes she accidentally still gives me her lunatic stare. 'Lena,' I say sternly. Her child's face grows uncertain, begins a hesitant smile. I think I'm the first person for many years she's dared smile at in this genuine way, admitting that the other mad stare is a protective act.

Already a month had passed when I began to ask different people with the most careful casualness, often letting several days pass between enquiries, about Lena. Last night I was remembering that first month. How far away it already seemed, so far that it was as if I was thinking not about my four-month-ago self but about a stranger. And one, incidentally, so stupefied with terror he'd been reduced to the acts and movements of a dummy. Logically my situation has hardly improved, so I suppose I've got accustomed to it — hardly a reassuring thought.

These memories occurred to me at the moment when I'd completed my reconnaissance. I'd reached a climax, a turning point, call it what you like. Directly ahead lay my first opportunity for real action. Till then I'd assumed that many practical problems would intervene, but instead I found none that I couldn't easily overcome. I was left with a single simple straightforward choice — and I had no idea what to choose.

I'd set out at eleven. Though summer is advancing quickly now, the evenings long and warm, the streets often full of people strolling together in the twilight, suddenly an hour after sunset they're deserted and silent except perhaps for the distant howls of some band of

Youth League returning from a group orgy. I could hear some of these creatures last night far away in the direction of the war cemetery, and as I hurried softly down the dark sides of streets towards open country I had a vivid picture of them hurling stones at prominent crosses, flinging about vases of flowers placed on graves by mourners, terrorising the gatehouse porter who'd locked himself in his cottage.

Soon I'd left the houses and was making my way over fields, past small spinneys, under a high and helpful moon, in the direction of that lit-up snake I'd seen months before, rattling distantly across this flat land. The early part of my route was familiar, leading me towards the arterial road, a route I'd taken on many nights in spring. I'd been going steadily for a couple of hours before I had my first sight of my objective.

There it was, perhaps a kilometre down stream, spanning the river in three arches, so brightly lit by the near full moon it seemed two-dimensional. It was somehow perfect, like a toy or model, all the low shabby buildings which by day probably clustered round its ends now hidden. But unlike the model we'd been shown during training the real thing had scale. It was enormous. The idea of destroying something so — godlike in its massiveness and perfect proportions produced in my mind a strange mixture of desire and terror.

Fifty feet below me — I was on a low scrub-covered bluff — lay the Gar, a familiar name since school geography days, but also entirely different from the Gar I'd then imagined, not just because of its greater width and more impressive sweeping curves, but for its speed. Because when I looked closely I noticed that the surface of this huge river, the largest I'd ever seen, was continually flickering in the moonlight. All those millions of tons of water weren't progressing to the sea with ponderous dignity but in a rushing-torrent, as headlong as a little stream.

I'd always assumed that the approach must be from this, the north bank. Not only was the southern approach much further from Urbville, but that bank was a restricted zone, which it would be difficult to enter. The purpose of my reconnaissance was to discover how this northern end was guarded. Moving with bent knees and hunched shoulders along ditches and behind low hedges I came closer. I began to detect a lighted area ahead. Lifting my face, I peered at last through the leaves of the final barrier. Instead of the guardhouse, sentries and searchlights I expected I found myself staring at a lone but biggish wooden signal box.

It was from the window of this, which stretched all across its ten-metre front, that the light came, illuminating clearly the last stretch of double track before the bridge. Inside the box, among banks of wheels and rows of huge levers like giants' hand-brakes, the signalman sat drinking tea and reading a newspaper.

For five minutes I stayed staring both ways along those tracks which reached in opposite directions into the dimness of bridge and countryside, still looking for some moonlit sentry or black hut with barbed wire. I could see none. I should have felt triumphant: such luck was better than I'd dared expect. Instead I was worried and apprehensive. Either I was missing something or it was the behaviour of a side so sure it was winning it had almost stopped trying.

Back again a kilometre up stream where I'd had my first view of those fine moonlit arches I tried to see in my imagination something my mind might have recorded but passed over. I still saw nothing. To act or to wait? To risk myself in this now clearly feasible operation or go on saving myself for that primary target towards which I was making such slow progress? It was this question my mind refused to take hold of but kept slipping off to recreate that first terrifying month of my mission.

For three days after my arrival in town I behaved like a rabbit that has found a burrow, any burrow, and won't move out however close the ferret comes because its fear of the open is far greater even than its fear of those red eyes in the darkness. I stayed in my room.

Even when I did at last leave I seemed to act not because of some reassertion of my courage or memory of the rightness of our cause; least of all because of some reviving hope as a result of my apparent reprieve — on the contrary, the longer I stayed there the more convinced I became that I was a fragment of some far wider disaster we had suffered. I went because I had to go, there's no other way to describe it. I went and waited at the factory employment office, holding out my papers, astonished that the terror inside me wasn't plain to everyone who saw me.

Getting my job had always been the part of my mission which had most alarmed me — after the drop itself. At any moment from that night onwards I might be stopped by a patrol and questioned. A casual mistake of speech, a message paper I'd forgotten to burn or slip into a cigarette, a hundred other tiny errors might put me instantly in far worse danger. But these were the slips which destroy most agents in the end and can never be totally guarded against nor imagined in detail. When I applied for work at the factory I was exposing myself intentionally to a danger which I could clearly picture.

I remember best the moment when the machine-shop foreman, as I later learned he was, held my papers and stared steadily at me as he tried to decide whether to believe them. I needed to act with refinement showing some alarm because anyone asking for a job is nervous, but not too much. I let him look at me and my papers alternately for perhaps thirty seconds, then began to explain quite unnecessarily that my movement permit showed two stamps because one was from my last employer and one from the town police. In fact there are always two stamps, which he knew but I pretended not to know. I made a good job of my anxiety, going on trying to make him listen even when he'd grunted that it wasn't important. Though looking back I've wondered whether I was more alarmed than I need have been. It's possible that he was a sympathiser.

This seemed more likely a few weeks later when I didn't see him at work one morning. That afternoon I heard he'd had a heart attack. Next day someone called it a breakdown and claimed to have visited him in the nearest Hospital for Social Diseases — as the nut house is now named — where they'd found him unable to talk properly, perhaps not even able to recognise them. Since then I haven't heard him mentioned and it's many months since a new machine-shop foreman took his job.

Even more significant, at that first interview he never questioned my cover story which my papers hinted at but didn't detail. I had a doctor's certificate to support my movement permit, with a certain Dr. Frankel's signature on it which Ops had assured me even Dr. Frankel would find it hard to deny, particularly when his trusted secretary showed him my name convincingly inserted in his own card index of patients, and I was all prepared to explain how I'd been doing similar work in the north but had come south because my nerves wouldn't stand the bombing — when suddenly it seemed there was no need.

My second cover story, more convincing because not

entirely to my credit, I began later to let drop a fragment at a time to fellow workers, knowing that I mustn't be a person mysteriously without background, nor of course obsessive about telling it, but just a quiet chap who's had troubles and moved here to escape them.

Born in a northern seaside town — Ops chose one which has been heavily bombed, where they believe most churches and church records have been destroyed — I married a local girl, but had no children. Five years ago we moved inland and here were caught in the fighting during the retreat — which of course I remember to call the advance. For ten days our village lay between the lines and was shelled by both sides. My wife was almost certainly killed, but I went back to look for her and to re-open my café, ironically called Café de la Gare since the line had become a valley of bomb craters.

Here — it's now that I ask my fellow workers for secrecy, so making it hard for them to avoid leaking it — I dealt on the black market. What else could I do, under pressure from local collaborators who would otherwise denounce me and the local Youth League who might otherwise have broken my café apart? I even dealt with the Visiting troops. Difficult to avoid since they already often wore civilian clothes, not to provoke resentment. They aren't bad chaps, human like the rest of us, I say, the petit-bourgeois philosopher. One day I sold a packet of genuine tea to a Visiting sergeant. He was not only in a civilian suit but so drunk he might have started a fight. By morning he'd probably have forgotten where he got it.

The moment he'd paid I knew what a fool I'd been. The look he gave me as he left was sober and vicious. What right had he, I ask peevishly, to hate me as a traitor to my country when he wasn't even a fellow country-man?

He came again. I sold him more. The more I sold him the more evidence he had. He seemed to take pleasure in watching me fall more and more completely into his power. Genuinely drunk, he'd come in late and sit with his friends, sipping a cup of the dyed water I sold as legal tea, telling them about me through clenched teeth, staring at me for twenty minutes without stopping — his drunkenness wasn't of an uncontrolled, tumbling-about style, but heavy and mind-darkening.

'Let's find some real tea,' I'd hear him say. 'No tea? Not acquainted with my friend Claude?'

He began to ask for terrifying quantities, far more than I could supply, of other rationed goods. A day came when I had to refuse him, explaining that all my sources of a particular item were exhausted. He stared at me with astonishment, almost pity, that I should tell him such a lie.

All night I barely slept. All next day I waited in terror, not knowing what to expect. Late in the evening he arrived with several friends. They sat drinking and laughing aggressively together. Nothing seemed changed till they stood to leave when, passing by the counter, he invited me to an impromptu midnight party at his flat.

That evening's closing time was my last. Before midnight I was already negotiating with a contact for false papers and a new name. By dawn Claude Fiche, café proprietor, was dead and Alec Meyer, migrant factory operative, was hiking south.

It's an adequate story — more important, I know it so well that if I hesitate I'm confident I'll be understood not to be inventing but to be hunting for the right words to describe what I'm remembering. This has indeed become just what I am doing.

Under cross-examination I shall break down, attempt to revert to my first cover: nervous worker escaping from the bombs, then let myself be driven to my third story: that I'm a deserter from this country's defeated army. I'll admit that, hidden in my room behind the wardrobe, I have my army papers. It's the sort of superstitious thing deserters really do, as if they need to preserve this connection with the person they once believed themselves. What's more, I *do* have them hidden there, and they're genuine. That deserter was a young soldier shot and buried by our own troops during the retreat. Ops were alert to their need for the papers of such casualties even that early, especially if they were unmarried and came from remote areas.

Checking with his regiment will confirm my story. Even if they check with his relations I shan't be blown unless I'm actually brought face to face with them. As a deserter I wouldn't have tried to write to them.

For a month after I got my job, far from confiding my supposed past to fellow workers, I barely lifted my eyes from my bench. It was as if I still couldn't believe I'd managed it and if I looked up I'd see every one of them laughing at me for being such a stupid optimist. No wonder that first month I don't remember noticing Lena . . .

A knock far below me at the street door. Three floors down in this shabby old terrace house I now hear other soft bumps, then the light thud as the door is shut behind her. Suddenly — not for the first time — I'm tense in my chair. Once more I'm about to do the thing we were most sternly warned against during many security lectures: associate with a local popsy.

I'm hearing again Colonel Judd's voice, using this quaint expression, sounding as he always sounded, as if he was putting his feelings into words with pain and repugnance. I'm seeing again the long stern face and strangely unmilitary grey side-whiskers of Colonel Judd, head of Ops, man of a different age and morality, who always gave me the impression that he'd been shocked into walking paralysis by the mischance which had put him in charge of a clandestine warfare unit. He did his duty, perhaps as a result did it better than anyone else could have, but because he had no instinct to turn to, no fragment of personal feeling ever got into his words or actions and he seemed instead to clutch in a sort of living rigor mortis at the rules — the new rules — of our game. After three or four desperate, semi-articulate rasping noises, red in the face from the embarrassment every choking phrase was causing him, he'd scrape out in a dying croak, 'Tell 'em, Biggs.'

I'm hearing again Major Biggs, the voice of Judd whenever Judd's inner conflict became acute, telling us of the W/T operator who in the flurry of an unexpected search hid his one-time pad in the bra of his current mistress with whom he'd been disturbed—perhaps subconsciously hoping to prove that he alone had access to that private place. Unfortunately before she'd had time to dispose of it her next customer, a Visiting Secret Policeman, happened to notice that one of her breasts had a more crackly consistency than the other. More unfortunately, she was so terrified by what she'd done and so grateful to the policeman for handing it back to her — after photographing it — that she didn't dare tell the W/T operator what had happened and as a result he sent out two months of signals which the enemy understood as clearly as plain language. The week his pad ran out they arrested and shot him.

Colonel Judd would undoubtedly consider Lena a local popsy.

Any minute now I shall hear her steps on the stairs. I shall know they're hers because of the way they're sometimes running, tripping ones and sometimes long ones of several stairs at a time, as if she's playing a succession of child's games with herself none of which last more than half a flight. I'll hear her taking the last flight in such enormous steps she must be counting to see how few she needs — she has long legs anyway: her long smooth legs make me think of a young animal — a deer perhaps, or a new-born foal.

Tonight I'm not only going to continue my rash relationship with Lena. I've decided to recruit her.

2

INSTEAD a pause has followed. Now very faintly below I hear voices. Lena is being held in conversation by one of the Patrases. The gross young Mr. Patras? His skinny discontented wife? One of their five children? I'm anxious for Lena to come. Now I've decided what to do I'm impatient to do it.

Looked at another way I'll only be carrying out my instructions. We're meant to recruit sub-agents. Since we can't use mass persuasion to rebuild a spirit of resistance in this crushed people the selection of individuals who will rise when the day comes is the only way. In different circumstances I'd take the advice of my circuit on my choice. Things being as they are, it's my duty to trust myself. Alone I've been badly handicapped even in my information-gathering role. Now that the time has come for something more active . . .

I've considered Lena as a possible assistant ever since I noticed her behind the urns of the factory canteen and began to hear fragments of her story; how at sixteen both her parents were taken away — activists caught in some early purge; how she hid behind a pile of logs in their garden shed for three days, too terrified to come back to the empty house . . . From the first I had been looking for possible recruits, from the day of my arrival in this town and my discovery that I was more completely alone than I'd ever imagined, the day I came closest to despair.

It dawned hopefully when I woke in the forest of young oaks where I'd spent a cold night on a bed of fairly dry leaves. All round me there was frenzied bird song. I lay still, not wanting to disturb this frenetic singing which not only stretched away in every direction but was coming from individual birds in bushes only a few feet away, now to my right, now to my left, now immediately behind my head. Though it was only March, I never remember so strong a sense that spring was here at last, not to be lazed about in but to be made use of before it was too late.

I rose quickly, ran my stolen bicycle deep into a near-by pond, glad to be rid of that mechanical abortion which had blistered my arse for a hundred kilometres and agonisingly compacted my coccyx for the last ten because of a flat tyre, and began to sort through the contents of my two cases, poor Bio's and my own. In the end I left both, packing into them Bio's transceiver, Kitch's gelignite, detonators, grenades and carborundum dust and my own unarmed combat wire, forged currency, spare Luger clips and the bulk of my pills, finally topping them with those layers of clothes which gave one just a chance of surviving a superficial search. The only incriminating articles I took were my Luger itself in its shoulder holster and my single capsule hidden in my lapel — the one Major Biggs called our hey-ho tablet. There was something particularly irritating about the way Biggs ended several of his security lectures with the smug words, 'At that point, gentlemen, the best advice I can give you is to consume your hey-ho tablet.'

That day which had begun so tunefully soon turned sour. The oak wood with its stony desiccated soil proved a bad place to bury two medium-size suitcases. For half an hour I bashed it with flints, jarred my toes by kicking at it, filled my fingernails with grit by scraping at it, and then only did a poor job. Shaving in the same pond, using its surface as a yellow mirror, my hands were so shaky I sliced my cheek. At last I emerged on to the road to discover with shock how close I'd come in the night to my destination. Low rows of houses were plainly visible on the skyline. Above these rose a few workers' apartment blocks and an occasional church spire, while to the right stood the furnace chimneys of Urbville's industrial estate. Certainly I was too close to hunt for a village station and take a train to the centre of town, thus avoiding the patrols which so often operate on town outskirts, though perhaps my near-disastrous mistake of three days earlier which had driven me to steal my bicycle might anyway have dissuaded me.

It had been my first foreign dawn, and I'd walked with a confidence I didn't feel into the ticket hall of the first station I'd found, calculating I was at least ten kilometres from the drop zone and doing something so rash it might not have been anticipated — even if they knew that one of us had survived. It took me some time to find a porter to ask when the booking office opened. He looked at me with surly suspicion. It was Sunday. Didn't I know that Sunday morning trains no longer ran, and only a skeleton service on Sunday afternoon?

Presently as I walked and the early spring sun rose to warm me I became a little light-headed, perhaps from hunger. I seemed to float forward and my legs, though still propelling me, grew numb. It was a surprise but of a curiously neutral sort to find that I'd passed through the suburbs without incident and was already in the grey and grandiose central square.

I sat at a café, bought a cup of coffee substitute and began to notice the people. These were the first I'd seen close-to — on the side roads along which I'd cycled there had been few cars and I'd kept well clear of the occasional peasant working in field or vegetable patch. At first I was disappointed. Their expressions were reasonably content even if preoccupied, and they seemed well enough fed and dressed. Our blockade must have been having less effect than we'd been told. But gradually I saw below these superficial exteriors all and more than I'd expected. How terrifying that propaganda could so totally destroy the good qualities these people had once possessed, persuading them to accept as normal the perverted values of the Visitors' system.

Key to this system was distrust and suspicion between people. Their anxious faces told me clearly how every one of them assumed that a big enough bribe would persuade even a close friend to inform on them. Split up by their personal greeds and fears, they had ceased even to want, let alone dare to fight together. Incredibly they'd been persuaded in a few short years that a fragmented society of this sort was right and desirable. They'd sunk even below the level of certain animals' societies: herds of horses, flocks of rooks, colonies of termites all lived with more mutual trust and co-operation. Here surely I was seeing a far more likely cause of humanity's eclipse than any cobalt bomb or world plague. Though I've later felt pity for them, the best of them, that morning I could only feel disgust as they passed each other in droves but would never look into each other's eyes.

I left the café, taking care not to over-tip in a currency I still wasn't familiar with. I began to walk to the first of my three contact points: 125 Avenue Georges. The mishap at the drop should have warned me of what was to follow, but I was still assuming it was an isolated catastrophe.

I even congratulated myself on having memorised the lay-out of the town's main streets, although at the time it had seemed an unnecessary precaution since the reception committee would bring us here and introduce us. The spring morning was still so early that although the sun in the country had seemed high and warm, in town it hadn't yet risen above the buildings. I shivered as I passed down streets of grey shadow which seemed to belong to a day many hours less advanced.

Avenue Georges had once been a street of residential houses built in a pompous classical style and many of these survived, some as houses, some as shops below and store rooms above, more as offices with the professional brass plates of doctors and solicitors on their doors. But in other places several had gone altogether and a concrete disaster been built instead. Walking down the even side of the street, I soon found that these changes were a problem, Many of the shops had no numbers, and often the new blocks would have a group number like 48–64. Nevertheless, peering across the street below its pollarded limes to those strong old panelled doors once attended by aproned serving maids I kept fair track of my progress.

I approached a side turn. Would 125 be this side or the other? The last building this side was the sort I've described: of bald angular concrete with wide concrete steps, glass revolving doors and a piece of scrap-iron sculpture on a plinth to one side. Above its entrance in sanserif capitals a motto was carved alongside the numbers 117–123. I passed across it and after ten more paces had also crossed the side turning — there was no equivalent turning on my side of the street. The first house on the opposite corner was numbered 127.

Shock kept me walking steadily forward. At the end of the street I glanced at my watch as if uncertain how to fill time before an appointment, then began to stroll back down Avenue Georges. There was no doubt about it: number 125 was missing.

Had Ops made a numerical slip? Even if I'd thought this likely it suggested a daunting number of alternatives: 127? 135? 225? Or had the street numbers been changed, every number from 127 onwards being increased by two? I allowed myself one further walk up Avenue Georges, this time on the uneven side, peering as closely as I dared at those brass numbers for marks left by earlier ones or patches of fresh paint to hide such marks. Detecting neither, I turned quickly back towards the town centre. If this had indeed been done, the street was almost certainly being watched for anyone who looked lost as he hunted for a missing house.

Shaken, but not really worried, I set off for Café Olympique, my second contact point. Streets *do* have missing numbers, I told myself, especially when there has been demolition and rebuilding, or when a house has been removed to allow for a side turn.

This café was in a poorer part of town close to the station among small grocery stores, coal merchants' offices and timber yards. It was missing too, though in another sense. A hundred metres away and long before I'd exactly located it my eyes settled on a gap in the low line of buildings, crossed by blackened beams above a rubble of broken glass, tiles, bricks and half-buried kitchen stoves and refrigerators.

The fire was recent enough for the pavement still to be fenced off and a small crowd of people to be standing across the street staring at it, though most were passing without a glance. I joined these six or seven watchers and soon discovered the answer to the question I preferred not to ask them: sagging across the blackened headboard of this burnt-out building's display window was a smashed sign of hollow glass with a bulb dangling in its cavity, and clearly readable on the unbroken portion of this were the letters 'OLY . . .'

'Some bomb,' I muttered to a short man in raincoat and hat.

'You're telling me!' he said, not looking at me, leaving me unsure whether he too was being ironic.

Fifty yards beyond I saw the official version. A blue police notice read, 'DANGER BROKEN GAS MAIN KEEP CLEAR.'

Significantly, though typically, people weren't keeping clear. Again and again in the months since that first morning, I've noticed that they are no longer expected to accept the literal meaning of official orders and news bulletins. A curious compromise has been reached in which the honour of the Visitors is satisfied if they display in public their version of the facts or of the orders they want obeyed and the population don't actually shout out the truth or flaunt their disobedience. It's a compromise in which the Visitors are winners every time, used calculatingly I believe, to give this defeated people a false sense of freedom.

Half an hour later I was passing the front of 'DISQUE SNAX'. My third contact point stood undamaged just where I'd expected it. For some reason this caused me greater alarm than either of my previous discoveries. I passed and repassed it, unable to decide whether to enter. In this business we learn to trust instinct as much as logic, so much more easily distorted by our hopes. By now, exhausted and slightly confused, I saw those fizzy drink advertisements, blue circles with crude red letters one on each side of the café's name, as goggling eyes. Below them the window of the bar was of dark green glass, through which I saw vague movements which I couldn't for certain distinguish from reflections. Three or four times I approached but at the last moment swerved away. At the fifth or sixth attempt I forced myself forward and in. A little dizzy, I stood at the bar, sipping a glass of what they still call wine but has the unmistakable flavour of fermented chemicals.

I spoke to the barman about the cost of food, the low quality of today's manufactured goods, the recent failure of the provincial football team . . . How simple plans seem at a distance and how easily they can be wrecked by tiny details. Here, on the point of making my first contact, I was blocked by the difficulty of deciding whether he *was* merely the barman or the proprietor. His fashionable flower-embroidered waistcoat, maroon shirt and stiff white collar — dowdy I guessed in any brighter light than this bar's dimness — were classless. But no other man was serving, and I was beginning to take risks, in the way we were warned we might, less because of physical tiredness than because of an emerging desire to escape by failing. Casually I dropped the password. 'Been a hard winter.'

At once he was giving me an intense stare. Instead of those words I longed for: 'Better than last year', there was a terrifying silence. He even seemed to be ignoring other customers' calls for service.

Was he so amazed to see me, when he already knew of our disastrous drop, that the answer had gone out of his head? Guessing that one of us had been captured and talked, did he believe I was a police agent, only waiting for his code reply to arrest him? Or was he indeed only the barman, reacting with genuine astonishment to a meteorological verdict so far from the facts? Yet again, had the real proprietor suffered the same eclipse as 125 Avenue Georges?

All these possibilities, hurrying through my mind, were interrupted by a sudden acute pain in my thudding heart. Several times I'd had slight pain there during those first two nights which I'd spent cycling on amphetamine. I'd taken a final dose before setting out for town and now, topped up by massive adrenalin secretions, it seemed to cause me a far more acute spasm. I held my chest with both hands and lowered my head to the bar.

At once the barman and a female glass-washer had arrived on either side of me. I was being carried into the kitchen and laid on a sofa. My face was being wiped with a cool damp cloth. Another man with handle-bar mustachios stood near. Dimly I congratulated myself. I was in the presence of the real proprietor. 'Been a hard winter,' I murmured, rashly impetuous now I was no longer in public.

'Kind of wandering,' the waistcoated barman said.

'Case for the ambulance,' the mustachioed man said.

That jolted me to my senses. I knew what the ambulance meant. Dizzy and still in pain, I sat up quickly, shaking my head. If these people were indeed my contacts they now dared do no more than warn me I could no longer trust them.

Swaying heavily, I came into the street. The bright sun, risen above the house roofs, dazzled me. It took concentration, weaving like a drunk, to reach the nearest café where I sat to recover.

One final address remained. We hadn't been told to memorise it because we'd been introduced there by the local circuit, but I found I knew it. It was the house of a sympathetic family called Patras who would give some of us lodging. No alternative remained but to approach them direct.

The door was opened by the person I now know as the younger Mr. Patras, a slug-like man of thirty-five at most, who I at once distrusted.

'I'd like a quiet room, preferably with a basin.' This is the code request for lodgings. It requires an answer in exactly the correct words: 'Depends what you mean by quiet.'

'Don't know what you mean by that,' this person said offensively, as if I'd insulted his room or his mother. Though so young, he had a gross oval of suspended flesh round his jaw.

All the time I inspected this room where I now live and bargained about price and the times when the bathroom would be free, I was considering whether to offer him the second code check. Was he merely so lazy he hadn't troubled to remember the exact words? If so, should I anyway trust him? Presently though all was fixed he still stayed in my room, like a porter waiting for his tip. 'Been a hard winter,' I suggested.

He gave me a short sour laugh and went out. What did that mean?

My reception here, culminating in this bitter laugh, such a contrast with the one Ops always managed to hint at, of immediate smiles and handshakes and a rapid descent to a cellar full of bombs, maps, gelignite and stens, shocked more than anything till then.

I guessed that this family, like that mustachioed proprietor of Disque Snax, was genuine, that these were indeed the people some of us had been meant to lodge with. Apart from the name, their whole house and style of living confirms my guess by its air of permanence. Cupboards, spare rooms and landings are littered with broken, once-valued, shoddy objects, from children's tricycles to old sacks through which onions sprouted several years ago. Though the enemy is thorough, he is surely not that thorough. But I guessed that although they had once been sympathisers, our cause had suffered such a disastrous setback that they could only sneer at someone like myself who reminded them of their past dangerous idiocy. Soon, I guessed, they'd consider it safer still to denounce me.

Sometimes in the evenings the Patrases invite me down to drink instant coffee substitute with them and watch television. These are the people I'm fighting to free, I think, people who live only to eat and sleep and have comfortable sensations, who from sloth or fear have given up.

When they aren't slothfully comfortable they squabble. Their minds seem full of ill towards each other. If their five children fight, young Patras and his wife find in this fresh material for their own life-long battle. They seem to suffer a grinding resentment for some injury they have done each other and this continues all day between every one of them. Surely it's connected with their 'occupied' status. If they weren't blinded by such preoccupations wouldn't they rise up in a body, screaming with indignation? Better die at once with dignity on the machine-guns than bit by bit of this snarling miserable disgust at themselves.

Indignation with the system which reduces them to such a condition is what I ought to feel — television, the lottery, the races, newspapers full of supposed news to keep them nicely balanced between greed, jealously and fear — and I try to concentrate on Grandfather Patras, the only one of them I like. He won't read newspapers — there's no other reading matter in the house — or look at television, his excuse being he's shortsighted and can't afford new glasses. Instead he keeps up a constant conversation with his smelly old dog, usually quiet enough not to provoke them, but loud enough for them to catch its tone. Sometimes I think they suspect that he and his dog are barracking them, sometimes that he's exchanging sentimental affection with it. Both make them mad. Suddenly all together like some infuriated pack they start shouting at him to keep quiet and stop spoiling their enjoyment. Terrible dismay comes on his face, so genuine that they have to believe it and this makes them still more angry.

But they must half respect and be a little frightened of him or they wouldn't let him keep his dog. New dog licences have been made impossibly expensive and though an old one can be extended at the former price till the dog dies there's much propaganda against people who don't voluntarily surrender such wasteful creatures to the national protein plants. When broadcasts of this sort, called 'Natural Resources' documentaries, are shown, I've actually seen the Patrases turn down the sound as if scared of what might happen if anyone ever seriously threatened to take his dog away . . .

Long ago Lena has arrived. She knocked softly and I let her in. We didn't touch or say one word to each other — this is our habit. We just watched each other — became acutely aware of each other's physical presence, is a better description.

Now she sits on the mat in front of the empty fireplace, knees up, soft pale arms wrapped round them, each hand gripping the other arm halfway to the elbow. What is she thinking? It's a question I often ask myself about people, knowing from the complexities and irrelevancies of my own thoughts that I'm unlikely to guess right. But about Lena, improbable as it seems, I sometimes think I do guess: she's not thinking anything. She's keeping her mind empty, waiting to hear what I think.

I open my mouth to tell Lena all that I mean to tell her tonight — and postpone it, hearing again those moments of low conversation in the house below.

I try to reassure myself. Even since I've known her I've been checking her, in the way our training makes instinctive. I've set traps for her: threads she'll break if she touches my radio, dust patterns she'll disturb if she hunts among the papers on my chest of drawers. By going to the bathroom I've left her alone with them. She's never fallen into them.

But I also remember an evening when she seemed unusually anxious to be back at her lodgings before the curfew — laxly enforced at that time — and I slipped out after her.

It was one of those dark windy nights with driving rain squalls, reminding me of the winter so recently ended, so soon to come again. Sheltering in a porch from one of these I almost lost her, then saw her far off moving fast below a semi-blacked-out streetlight — fortunately she was wearing a white mackintosh. Though it was hard to be sure at such a distance I thought she was running.

I ran too, but long before I reached that streetlamp I'd again lost sight of her. Suddenly, on the far side of the street, she was sitting in a café window. It was one of those cafés which stay open hours later than the rest though they do little business, as if their owners have so completely run down they haven't even the energy to close. From where I stood I could see the back of the head and

28

shoulders of this owner, keeping very still as if his eyes were attending to some difficult calculation his hands were doing out of sight on the bar top.

So Lena hadn't gone home, as she'd said. There could be many innocent explanations for that: a soaking scud of rain might have given her an impulsive need for a cup of coffee substitute. She accepts the fact that her life is directed by a succession of impulses more than most of us do, with our need to pretend we act rationally. Or she might have pretended she was going home to conceal from me some other (but non-political) relationship — with this café owner for example, whose heavy shoulders I could see through his rain-distorted window. Though he and Lena were three metres apart, not talking to each other, I could imagine how they might already be in some rather touching relationship which was helping him bear a lonely life with a bitchy wife.

I came closer. The rain had stopped and for a moment there was no wind though I could still hear it moaning distantly above the roofs of other parts of the town. Quickly I crossed to the pavement in front of the café itself, thinking a lamp standard would conceal me. I had just time to discover that it didn't and that instead the light from the café window was falling fully on to me so that from the inside I'd be a clearly visible figure against blackness, when a far door of the café opened and a second man in a dark overcoat entered. At once Lena stood and came out, passing close by him. It was lucky that another soaking squall came driving up the street; also that I'd put on a sou'wester of black oilskin which she wouldn't recognise and I now pulled low over my forehead against the rain. She passed so close to me that I heard her mutter 'Shit' at this violent gust which blew her white coat open, but she didn't recognise me.

With determination I push the whole of that worrying but inconclusive incident aside.

'Lena, you must listen carefully.'

3

My confidence in her soon returned. I'd been right to trust her.

She didn't say much. She never does. At first she just stared as if she suspected I was teasing her, or as if she still didn't dare believe me. Suddenly she did believe me. She grew very excited.

Naked on the floor, cross-legged Buddhist style, a look of idiot complacency on her face, she sat wagging a finger left and right in front of her eyes like a metronome. Someone sitting on a ticking land-mine?

All that evening moments of doubt returned to her and she'd stare at me with questioning eyes as if asking whether I really meant it. Those I could handle. The ones when she believed me were harder. Now, tonight? she wanted to know. I had to dampen her enthusiasm, explaining that these things needed careful planning. I'd give her details as soon as I'd worked them out. But her look of disappointment warned me that if she felt our first operation was less than imminent she might be slipshod about security.

'Quite soon,' I said.

I didn't mention the factory. There'll be plenty of time for that. The other comes first — if it's successful it will be a signal to Ops that I'm still alive and becoming active — the only kind of signal left to me.

When Lena and I made love that night we were giggly, almost hysterical. We had to keep hushing each other in case we woke the Patrases. On top of her, trying to spread her long fair legs and come into her, she was still making it into some strange sabotage charade, suggesting perhaps that she wasn't having any detonator inserted *there* . . .

The only sort of signal left to me. As soon as Lena had gone I connected my aerial and once again began to call Ops. For three minutes, as long as I dared, I went on asking for a Transmit Signal. I've ceased to expect one.

I sent my message. 'AJAX CALLING AJAX CALL-ING ABSENCE FURTHER ORDERS COM-MENCING OPERATIONS PER FIELD BRIEFING.' Silence followed.

I'd inserted the necessary bluff check and true check errors, but of course they were Bio's. Once again I wondered whether their silence might be because they were receiving Bio's checks in a fist which is clearly not Bio's — though they taught me the elementary use of a transceiver, they took no record of my fist.

But it's not a satisfactory explanation. Even if they suspect that I have been captured, have confessed the checks and am being impersonated — the enemy selecting me rather than Bio just because my fist was probaby unre-corded — they would still reply. False information sent under the impression that it was being believed could help us as much as real information . . .

I recovered my suitcases three days after I'd established a base here to which to bring them. Travelling on a local bus — less conspicuous than walking — I looked out across the flat, devastated countryside. On my first walk into town I'd failed to notice the extent of this devastation because the newly risen sun was giving every building distorted shapes and shadows. Now, wherever I looked I saw sagging barns, broken machinery and even occasional sections of wall jutting alone from seas of tumbled brick. My cases, buried between the two oak saplings I'd nicked, were intact, though damp had soaked through the bottom of one, made as it had to be of local shoddy imitation leather. If I had a better knowledge of radio I would know for certain whether this damp could have damaged my transceiver.

I set it up at the back of my chest of drawers, plainly on view but not absurdly prominent. Equipment has much improved since the early days of the fifteen-kilo B mark IIs which clearly showed themselves for what they were. This set is almost as small as the old A mark IIIs and has the far more important advantage that it looks superficially like a normal radio. Any examination of its works would at once tell an expert what it was, but a snooping landlord will probably pass it by if it's casually exposed which he wouldn't if he found it in a bottom drawer.

My next need was an aerial, at least twenty metres long, preferably rising above roof level. Late that night I set out to solve this problem. My room is on the top floor of the house, but from the street I'd noticed that there was a dormer window in the roof above. Its cracked glass repaired with strips of brown paper suggested an attic, and I guessed that access might be through a trap door in the passage outside my room.

Standing on a chair I raised this trap, heaved myself with a struggle and the bruising of a hip into the space above, hauled up the chair on which I'd placed the coiled aerial and shut it below me. Crouching silently, I listened for sounds of any curious Patrases coming to investigate the odd bumps I'd made.

The darkness was so thick around me it seemed touchable, a solid substance which I'd thud against as soon as I moved. It smelt of dust. At last I dimly saw the dormer. Quickly I focused my eyes ten degrees to the right to get the image off the yellow spot on to more sensitive parts of my retinas. At once its grey Gothic shape became twice as distinct.

I crept towards it, taking care not to tread on the laths and end with my legs dangling into a room below, as a parlour maid of my uncle's once had, thus revealing her nightly rendezvous with the garden boy — I still have a clear picture of those black-stockinged legs suggesting sausages projecting helplessly through the plaster. I forced the window open and climbed out. Standing upright on its outer sill, I hoisted myself on to the slate ridge above.

Now I could reach to the ridge of the house itself and had soon pulled myself up there. Sitting astride, I had a good view of a largish section of town.

The first thing I noticed was how dim the streetlights were. From above they suggested dark mushroom tops which gave no direct upward light but only a glow around their edges. I was relieved. I'd been depressed to think that the town took so few black-out precautions, deducing that at this distance inside enemy territory our bombers were no longer a danger.

These lights shone down on deserted streets, as I'd have expected during curfew. Occasionally I could hear a patrol car cruising somewhere near but I never saw one. Looking away above the lights and the nearest roofs, I saw a dark mass of foliage — the tops of the plain trees in Urbville's central square. Beyond this my factory, standing among several others in the industrial estate, was clearly visible. I saw its tall chimney and its extensive machine shops where the second night shift would now be at work. More prominent than these dark blocks was its administrative building. For the first time I got an exciting shock of conviction. They hadn't exaggerated: it was enormous, quite out of proportion to the factory it was supposed to administer.

My attention was distracted by a distant rattling sound. Somewhere out in that flat land an express train was hurrying through the night. Faint and far off though it was, I was able to imagine the great roaring, straining, energetic thing it would be close to. I'd just decided that it must be travelling blacked-out, since it was almost certainly in my field of vision when it appeared, perhaps from some cutting, now suggesting a busy lighted serpent.

All right, I told myself, I was stuck with a dated idea of war: black-out was no protection against rockets. Equally, their early-warning radar might now be so reliable they could leave the blacking-out of items like city streets and trains which were under direct state control till danger was near. That brightly lit express still disturbed me.

I worked myself along the roof ridge to the chimney stack. Gripping it and standing, I tied one end of my aerial as high as I could reach up the house T.V. aerial. I tied it again to the iron bracket which held the T.V. aerial to the chimney stack then, guessing roughly the position of my window, I tossed the rest of the coil outwards and sideways to hang into space. Unfortunately the wire's weight dragged it back and it came to rest running vertically down the roof slope. I began to pull it in to try again. It grew taut, jammed by the gutter or in some slate crevice.

Ten minutes later, back in my room, rather breathless and with my hip more painfully bruised, I turned out the light and peered out of the window. I could see nothing.

But it must be there, about five metres away if my estimate was right. And there it would be in the morning, dangling from the eaves, perhaps reaching to the pavement.

Leaning out of the window, I gripped the gutter and tested it with my weight. It creaked and sagged. I seemed to feel this sagging grow into an accelerating fall and grabbed wildly at my window frame to save myself ... pure imagination.

I took the cord I'd made from twisted string and passed it round the gutter, then round my body under my arms. Cautiously I climbed backwards through the window and let it take my weight. Again there was a scarey creaking above my head. 'All bark and no bite,' I told myself — the sort of idiotic phrase of comfort which comes into one's head at such moments. Little comforted, I began to move sideways along the face of the building.

My method was to take my weight with my left hand, rapidly shift the cord along the gutter with my right, allow it to tauten again and swing sideways till I was suspended below its new position.

About the seventh time I performed this manoeuvre my sideways swing caused a terrifying cracking sound immediately above my head as if bricks, mortar and pieces of iron were popping free from each other. Desperately I hung on, expecting at any second to feel myself lurch into space. Far below I heard the impact of a biggish piece of masonry which must have broken free, then the multiple rattle of its fragments skittering away across the pavement. My sense of the black twenty-five metres below me was acutely revived by the long seconds which that piece of masonry had taken to reach the ground and by the splintering sound of its impact. Drenched with sweat, I was shivering so heavily I would certainly have fallen but

35

for the cord. At this moment I suddenly saw my aerial, hanging unnoticed only a metre to my right.

It calmed me. The gutter seemed to be holding. With enormous caution I reached sideways with a foot and hooked it.

Holding it in my mouth, shivering and sweating continuously, I worked my way back towards the window. Presently I was sitting on the floor of my room, taking the deep breaths we've been trained to take on such occasions. I'd been out there seventeen minutes.

Now when I need my aerial I can bring it in, but at other times I lay it in a neat coil in the section of gutter immediately above my window — I feel confident the Patrases are not gutter-cleaners. I've calculated that a cloudburst would extend the coil in the other direction, not wash it back out of reach again.

I've grown accustomed to transmitting into silence, but I wasn't at first. How well I remember my hopes when, my aerial connected, I sent out my first call. All the time I made the final adjustments I told myself not to hope too much: they weren't likely to be listening at this particular moment. At once I got the answer I'd prayed for — 'AJAX TRANSMIT'.

I transmitted. My relief made me verbose. After the two checks, which I'd carefully prepared, I sent all six sentences I'd coded but meant to keep for different transmissions, knowing the danger of long messages. Silence followed. I got no 'MESSAGE RECEIVED' signal. I never have.

I'm still convinced I received that first transmit signal. Otherwise I would have gone on asking for it. Some valve must have collapsed as soon as it was used. But I can't help also occasionally wondering whether I have somehow transformed one of the many times I've imagined, even dreamed, of receiving it into what seems a real memory.

Our ordinary broadcasts are different. I can hear these on medium wave, though so badly jammed I can make little sense of them. The set is designed to perform in this way, just like a normal old-fashioned radio. Can it possibly have a fault which affects reception on certain wavelengths only?

Once a week I visited a different shop with a valve for exchange. If I replaced them all I must sooner or later replace the broken one. Lucky, I thought, that they hadn't forbidden the sale of all radio spares except those for their V.H.F. sets which can only receive local stations. But after I'd sent several shopkeepers burrowing into ancient drawers at the back of their store rooms I suddenly realised that they might be still allowing the sale of such parts for a good reason: to check who wanted them. By then only two remained unreplaced and I'd already begun to suspect that something more basic was wrong.

Till I got to know Lena a part of my nights was always spent with my set. Late in the evening when quiet had settled on the streets outside and on the Patrases below, I'd transmit a summary of my observations of the last twenty-four hours. Troop and traffic movements. Aircraft sighted. Assessments of the local population's morale. Technical details from the factory. I never again fell into the error of a long message, so risking a fix by their mobile direction-finders.

Then I'd tune to the B.B.C., but it was so jammed I often got little except the sense of a distant voice speaking my own language. At least we were still there, fighting on, I'd tell myself, though a more alarming theory has gradually crept up on me: that we aren't still there, that we've been defeated, that these broadcasts are coming from their side because the sense of an enemy presence suits them.

It's a theory supported by the fact that the news is more heavily jammed than amusement programmes, which would be less likely to contain propaganda. Of these, the one I listen to with the greatest frustration is Family Choice because, if it genuinely comes from home it's this programme which is passing to our agents their instructions, coded as record choices from sweethearts to lovers at the front or from grandchildren to grandparents in hospital. 'Elsie of Bognor Regis, for Vivian, wherever he may be. *The Lambeth Walk*, with all my love.' Sometimes these messages excite me to frenzy. I write them down. I stare at them. I curse them aloud for their meaninglessness.

My cursing changes. It's Judd I'm fucking and buggering at, that whiskered dummy. What right has he to keep me here in such ignorance? Even if I was still in radio contact it would never occur to his stultified imagination to pass me the truthful news of the war which I miss so badly. In contrast to my cautious, secretive, observing existence, which I've almost grown to feel is a proper way to live, this lack of reassurance is infuriating, a sort of insult.

Though to be fair I, too, never imagined what such total isolation from the truth would be like; the pressure, like a temptation, to stop resisting and believe the lies I read every day in the local papers, accept the propaganda victories I hear reported every half-hour on the factory radio. Nor, of course, could I expect him ever to send me the information I would like most: when to expect the 'Rev', or 'Second Coming', as we would jokingly call the invasion.

There are days when I find myself standing quite still in the street, listening to the far-off drone of our approaching planes. But as soon as I become conscious of what I'm doing and listen more carefully I find I can no longer hear them. I've been imagining them.

Last night I'd barely completed my transmission when there was a knock at my door. I stood hurriedly, my eyes checking left and right for anything incriminating left exposed. Right hand inside my shirt front, gripping that hard reassuring butt, I opened the door with my left and moved back behind it, using it as a shield. No one strode in. No tramping boots and ankle-length greatcoat. Lena had returned.

Once more I took her to bed. She stayed the night — it's something we don't often risk but last night I knew I was right to give her this reassurance. Perhaps I needed reassurance too. Though we were now together in a new sense, she was only freshly committed to her long lonely fight against her society and I was reminded of my own earlier anguished sense of desertion.

I suppose I'd been so occupied with my transmission that I hadn't heard her ring the street bell and be readmitted by the Patrases. That was why I had the odd but improbable idea that she'd never left the house.

4

SHE presses me for action. Perhaps I should have waited to confide in her till nearer the time when I shall need her help. This time approaches but I'm reluctant to hurry it forward and am again checking my decision. The longer I leave it the safer it will be: after an act of sabotage the first thing they do is question every employer and landlord about recent arrivals.

More accurately, she doesn't press me because she instinctively knows how this would worry me but watches me with big childish eyes which tell me how she'd like to.

Last night, to calm her I described my first reconnaissance. Even to me it made the job sound suspiciously easy and I knew I had to go again. As soon as she left I set out.

Starting by that familiar route which led me towards the arterial road I found myself remembering almost with nostalgia those weeks in early summer when I'd come this way almost nightly. I used to reach the road itself soon after midnight, wrap myself tightly in every warm and waterproof garment I'd brought, settle into a ditch so that my head was as low as the grass and begin to count.

All night hundreds of lorries thunder down that arterial road. How crude they make the camouflage of earlier wars seem. These lorries are truly camouflaged, which means that only a practised observer can tell them from their civilian equivalents. They aren't even of a standard type, that would also be a crude error, making them easy to distinguish. Furthermore, the whole idea of distinguishing is based on a misconception, when in this total war every lorry *is* carrying war material. The cargoes of bombs or shells I might find inside would only be different in their tactical use from the cargoes of food pulp or shoddy, instant-collapse household machinery which is used to buy the co-operation of an occupied population.

Even better than those hours of watching and counting —when I'd sit so still I'd seem to become some strange cocooned presence, without limbs because I'd ceased to feel any of these, just eyes and a mind — I remember nostalgically my returns in those early summer dawns. Often I'd be late. I'd have such a strong urge to stay there in my cocoon that when I did break free and find that my outer mackintosh was running with dew and my hair sodden, I would realise that dawn was already in the sky. I remember the flat meadows I'd cross which were so drenched in moisture that my already moist trousers became clinging rags after a few paces. I remember the sense they gave me that they'd been standing like this all night with infinite neutral patience, not hostile, in the way pine woods can be, not in any hurry, just waiting quietly here for men, those noisy transient creatures to go away. Patient, neutral and somehow proper. A properness we might occasionally imitate.

When I went west to the other arterial road I'd cross a different hillier country and here, on similar sunlit mornings, I'd stand on rises looking across rolling hills and woods, every fold of which would be filled with its separate lake of mist. Trees on the intervening ridges would throw shadows right across these mist lakes, almost to the top of the opposite sides of the valleys. Five hundred metres of tree shadow. Often then, the whole sky would be full of wheeling, shrilling swallows. Stupid, I used to think, to imagine I wanted real nature which would be rock and gas for ever. I merely wanted earlier simpler forms of life like grass and trees and skimming birds.

Descending once into one of these mist lakes and moving along a small country lane, I remember having the impression that I was following someone. I seemed to see his grey shape quite clearly about twenty paces ahead of me. He grew clearer, I halted, glancing for a ditch to dive into. At that exact moment he also halted. I hurried softly forward to try to see what sort of person he was. At once he seemed to hurry too. Some effect of the mist projecting my own shape ahead of me — this scientific explanation satisfied me, even though I continued to be aware of his moving presence ahead until I reached the outskirts of the town.

Remembering these things I approached the north end of the bridge more directly than before and presently found myself peering from behind the same low hedge at that big wooden signal box with its single bright window and its signalman who tonight had both hands on one of those giant levers but was keeping quite still, as if listening for something in his head which would tell him when to pull it. For an instant all seemed as before, then it didn't. Far from alarm, I experienced relief.

Opposite the box and only a few metres to my left a bright searchlight on a pole poured a brilliant pool of light on to the final metres of track before the bridge. Either it was new or it hadn't been lit before. At exactly this point three-deep pyramids of coiled barbed wire now formed fences which came so close to each side of the tracks that they seemed barely to leave space for trains to pass between them.

I had just time to reflect that it made Lena more essential to my plan when I heard a well-known distant sound. Quickly it grew louder, changing from a far away clatter to an urgent chuntering roar. I turned and hurried back. I went so fast that I fell several times and ripped my hand on a fence. I hurried because it might be fitted with some bright searching beam which would light me up, but I now suspect I was also urged on by a strange reluctance actually to see this great thundering machine. Fifty yards away I crouched and hid my face as it crashed by, shaking the ground. It had half gone before I made myself look cautiously round and saw that it was loaded with troops.

High up there they were rushing through the night, window after window of them, identical grey-uniformed pairs in each. Not a seat was empty and the dim corridors beyond seemed crammed.

On my way home the big pale sinking moon reminded me vividly of another full-moon night, the night of our drop. Low over another wooded hill, it had looked startlingly similar as I'd come tumbling to earth, strapped helplessly in my harness amid such a clatter of small-arms fire, banging of grenades and whistling of lethal metal fragments that I'd given a bitter laugh. After all our planning and secrecy, this. Clear of the plane, I'd felt the jerk of my parachute above me, gone floating gently into darkness and experienced that fine moment of exhilaration many agents remember, partly relief that the bloody thing had opened, partly physical excitement at drifting in this silent cool air, partly a sense that I was free at last to behave as I saw fit without continual well-meant correction ... only to land at the centre of this gay firework display. Five seconds later — surely my longest — I was out of my harness and flat on my face in sand and heather.

Were there omens? I remember as we approached the drop zone counting the torches: three I'll live, five I won't . . . but this is the sort of childhood habit I often revert to under stress, and I forget how many I saw. Real omens, then? Judd's black plastic cape as he came from the airport mess to shake our hands and give us semi-articulate grunts of encouragement, an untypical smirk on his face, of satisfaction, I suspect, that the roar of the plane's engines was anyway making him inaudible? Or the fact that I never received that last letter from Jane, which I'd been expecting for a week?

I remember trying with all my strength to force myself lower into the resisting ground and the way half my mind

43

again laughed at this idiotic instinct. Presently, between explosions, above the whine and whistle of bullets I heard my name called. So at least one more of us had survived — or was it a trick? We'd been warned of such things.

'Ajax.'

Using my hands to grip the heather at its roots, I dragged myself forward on my belly. Trick or not, I had to investigate that call. Tracer whipped past above me. A bright light searched the ground. It seemed to find me. I lay rigid and hopeless. It passed on. A minute later I slid into a gully and at the same instant a grenade exploded on its opposite rim. In the flash I saw Kitch and Bio crouching and clutching each other, staring wide-eyed as in a press photo.

They angered me crouching there apparently shocked into paralysis. Through the racket I began to shout at them not to give up but help me think of a plan. As soon as I came close to them I was ashamed of my anger. They'd both been hit, Bio several times in the chest — dark froth was dripping from his chin — and Kitch in the thigh or groin where a wet black stain reached from his crotch to his left knee.

I think Bio was dying already. It was Kitch who gave me the two cases he'd recovered, Bio's containing the transceiver, and his own with carborundum powder, explosives and grenades. After that he drew his gun on me. I shrugged. In an instant we seemed to pass wordlessly through the whole range of objections and counter-objections and leave them behind.

The last I saw of them was from fifty metres along that low gully where I was creeping and dragging those heavy cases. A more violent burst of firing made me look back. Kitch was on his feet above where they'd been crouching, caught fully in the beam of a searchlight. He seemed to be holding up an arm as if calling to them. A moment later his body gave several violent jerks and at the same time began to collapse on itself as if it had been inflated. That was when, low over a near-by wood, I again noticed our landing moon still shining quietly down on the drop zone — with astonishment it seemed at the more than usually crazy way these humans were behaving.

Commander, wireless operator, explosives technician: a team of three, the Ops system — fine in theory but the loss of one deprives such a team of half its expertise. No wonder, seeing I lost two, I've felt a blundering amateur ever since.

I never saw Vim. Traitor? Victim of torture who confessed? I still don't know. He should have taken us south and introduced us to the rest of Detergent. I guess now that the whole circuit was already collapsing and that Ops also suspected it or they wouldn't have flown out Flash in a hurry the week before — another matter I keep simmering for Judd.

This morning I reached home before the moon had set. All was dark in the Patras rooms. Some mornings I've been so late that young Patras has been padding around in slippers and paisley imitation-silk dressing-gown, a pathetic pastiche of a man-about-town culled from T.V. escape comedies, comically inappropriate under his oval dewlap and cigarette-dangling mouth. I've had to give him a big wink. At once — with a sharpness in repulsive contrast to his gross and slothful body — he has got the message: I'm creeping home at dawn from the town brothel.

Tonight I shall give Lena details of the help I shall need from her.

I CAME into the street — she still wasn't due for half an hour and I needed bread. At once it was happening all around me.

The first burst came from so close behind my head I seemed to feel its blast. As I ducked and stumbled I believed for a fraction of an instant that I'd been hit. There he went, already near the far end, running hard.

The end of this street slopes uphill so I had a clear view of the thirty metres he still had to cover. His scampering legs were a pathetic contrast to the desperately slow progress he was making. It seemed impossible that he wouldn't be hit. Now the shots were running up the street beside him, raising little puffs of dust, suggesting some small animal scuttling along by his feet rather than high-velocity bullets fired from two hundred metres away. Other bursts were coming from street corners and from windows — it must have been a trap — and from an armoured car which lumbered into view between us. I couldn't breathe. For the first seconds I knew he had no chance but the nearer he came to the bend the more an unbearable hope forced itself on me and my heart thundered in my ears. At last he was beyond it.

I hurried too, not down the street he'd used but through a side lane into a parallel street which lead in the same direction. I believed he'd escaped. I heard and saw nothing. The streets were deserted, even the traffic apparently halted. I reached the building — an abandoned municipal office standing alone — only seconds after they have reached it. A group of three or four of them were close to its big old door, planting a charge perhaps.

At once there was a sharp burst of fire and they were running back except for one who lay on the top step, his legs giving convulsive kicks on the dusty stones. A few moments later a single rather innocent bang from the far side of the square told me they had changed their tactics. The mortar bomb, landing on its roof with a much louder report, sent tiles and laths flying upwards curiously suggesting that the explosion had been generated inside.

Circling quickly I reached a smaller square on to which I knew this building backed. By now three or four bombs had exploded. Already smoke from a fire was rising in a white column from the broken roof and I could hear the crackle of burning wood. As I'd hoped this smaller square was empty; either they didn't know of it or things had happened so fast I was ahead of them. I was about to try the rear door when, glancing upwards, I saw him.

The few windows in that building's back wall were dotted about without pattern, suggesting the added water closets of a sanitary reconstruction. At one of these he stood, the lower frosted panel hiding all except his neck and head, quite still, facing sideways. Whatever could he be doing?

Frantically I signalled, pointing downwards to the still unguarded rear door. He didn't or wouldn't see me. His thin grey face with short hair stayed turned sideways, preoccupied. I came closer. I searched the ground for pebbles. I waved more wildly. Suddenly, as if he'd known about me all the time but was only now free to attend, he stared directly at me, nodded and disappeared.

Five seconds passed, then ten — what was happening? Had he understood? All the time a great roaring sound came closer; that armoured car was grinding its way along one of the narrow lanes which ran down the building's sides. It reached the square just as he emerged.

He ran straight past me without a glance. At once the firing started. I ran too. Bravery is an odd thing. An official citation would say that I courageously attempted to draw the enemy's fire to allow him to escape. It didn't feel like that; more like the obvious next move in a game which that afternoon I was playing with a certain dash and skill.

Lena was waiting in the passage outside my room.

When she lets her hair out of that absurd white cap which is factory-canteen uniform, it's long and fair. It goes with her long pale but strong legs.

We sat together on the bed, sewing my charges — cleverly disguised in local soap wrappers — into two bandoliers made from a pair of her net tights. I didn't tell her about my near escape — as soon as I saw her I controlled my heaving chest and forced myself to take long even breaths. I still didn't know enough about it myself.

Who was he? Did he escape? Did it mean that there were still a few resistance workers active in this town and if so should I be moving into action before I'd made contact with them? I'd run after him in the hope of contacting him, but I was also irritated that he had waited till now to emerge, thus interrupting what I had spent so much time planning to do alone with Lena.

Instead I described to her my discoveries of the previous night. At once she grew more talkative than I've known her. My picture of some train containing perhaps a thousand soldiers dragging itself carriage by carriage from that bridge into the broad Gar seventy metres below, of their terrified screams as they realised they were falling, released a greater hate for them than I'd suspected. I begin to understand that she's been waiting the whole of her short life for someone who'll tell her how to funnel this hate into action. Alone she's felt powerless.

But she's survived. All attempts to brainwash her into believing that her parents died of food-poisoning, all their hints that their deaths were a deserved end for people buying black-market rations, have failed to break down her deep irrational conviction.

I feel aching pity for her — and an admiring wonder at the way she has refused to submit to their persuasion and reasoning. My own intellectual anger is belittled by her deep animal fury. She describes things I, too, have felt. Her motives are mine. Like her, I am bitter when I think of their conditioning systems, their propaganda machinery, the way they have made it almost impossible ever to discover truth. But she makes me realise that my resentment is more personal and selfish than hers. Though she has personally been more hurt than I have, she has transformed this into a general compassion for, and anger on behalf of all people.

The only thing they have done to me personally, I realise, is turn my only life, from which I once expected so much happiness, into this persecuted spying thing. And, bitter though this makes me, I am perhaps also glad to be able to blame them for what I would otherwise have had to blame myself. Illogically, I feel that they have shown me what life really is, making the other seem like a period of childhood innocence. Even my life with my pretty mistress Jane. That especially perhaps.

Did she write me that last letter, or did she somehow know that I'd already deserted her? Did she hear all those promises I made her — at Broadstairs, Southend, Burnham-on-Crouch. you name it, there I made them — of coming back safely to love her again as things it was necessary for me to say but connected only with the past and not the future . . .

When they found Lena they told her she'd been absurd to hide. She'd lost her last chance of seeing her parents alive. What she'd thought was terror on their faces as they heard the ambulance siren had been their stomach pains which they'd been hiding, not to alarm her. How had the ambulance known it was needed? To protect her, they'd called it from an upper room.

She'd been forced to see her parents in their glass-topped coffins. Because they'd been of managerial status they'd been given these — though they were no doubt slipped out of them for cremation. Looking down on them lying there so dead and unconnected with the people she'd loved, she'd felt only hate. Hate for them for abandoning her and for the Visitors for taking them away. She'd neither believed nor disbelieved their story. That wasn't the way her mind worked. She'd just felt deep injury and a determination somehow, sometime to make someone pay for it.

They'd sent her for treatment to the local hospital. Here, at the out-patients' clinic a psychologist had repeated to her week after week the official facts. She'd never contradicted them. An animal cunning had made her hide her obstinate refusal to believe, though she couldn't hide the wild looks and distracted acts which had made them send her there.

Presently she'd come half to like this psychologist, who did his work a little sadly. She'd even put his version of events and her conviction into a limbo together, rival answers which there was no need to judge between. After all she had little proof that her parents had been resistance workers, only her memory of those three days when she'd been in the garden shed and heard the continual crashing of hammers and splintering of wood in her empty house as the Visiting Police smashed the furniture and took up the floorboards in their search for evidence. It was a memory which had become more dreamlike the longer she'd kept it to herself. But by not discussing it she'd kept it safe, as if she knew that anyone who trespassed near might interfere with her determination some day to make someone suffer.

Later I took her to the curtained cupboard at the back of my room to give her a glimpse into my second suitcase: grenades, Luger magazines, pills, detonators ... I'd meant to shut it quickly, but she held the lid up, peering with fascination. 'What's this?' she asked, pointing to the coil of steel unarmed-combat wire.

For a second I didn't want to answer. 'We'll be needing that,' I told her, and saw again that signalman among his brake levers and wheels in that lit-up signal box, with his thick working-class neck.

My feelings for Lena grow deeper. Last night when I made love to her I felt a new anxious concern for her and new happiness that I was comforting her. At first I was continually aware of those mad stares and *non-sequiturs* which made other people judge her touched in the head. Either they've grown less common or I've stopped noticing them.

6

WE were visiting the local Hospital for Social Diseases. We'd borrowed two bicycles from the Patrases.

It had been in my mind ever since the disappearance of that machine-shop foreman, fitting so well with all we'd been told about the use of drugs and asylums in place of jail and torture. Lena's psychologist provided the entrée I'd lacked.

It was a last unexplored avenue of possible contact, but the chances were remote, and I might have left it unexplored except for a memory which had begun to haunt me: that long thin face with hair *en brosse*, turned sideways to a lavatory window, listening to the mortar bombs crashing above.

Early on, for example, I'd send a coded postcard to the neutral address they'd given me. It was for exactly my sort of emergency isolation that this had been intended.

I should have had an answer — a postcard from another friend or better still something by courier — in about two weeks. From the twelfth day my hopes rose. For three or four days I was acutely alert to every sound in the passage outside my room, watched every person I passed in the street for a sign. From about the eighteenth day I began to listen and watch less hopefully.

And I'd thought of neighbouring circuits which, unlike Detergent, might still be functioning. I'd had no briefing about them — it's a first principle to keep circuits isolated from each other so the collapse of one won't bring down the rest. But I'd once worked briefly on Ops staff — routine training to help a field agent see what he looks like from the other end — and managed a circuit which lay a hundred and fifty kilometres to the west of Detergent. A friend with a desk in the same office managed the intervening one: Additive.

I remembered him once telling me that M.S.G., the organiser of this circuit, used as his principal rendezvous a café in the town's main square where Visiting Troopers passed all day by the dozen, directly facing the town's central police station. I'd once even seen M.S.G. when he'd been temporarily flown out and remembered a heavy tall mackintoshed man with a big Roman nose.

On an early Sunday morning, one of my first free days since getting my job, I took the bus for Durville, around which Additive operated. Once more the drab flat countryside showed the devastation it had suffered in that one terrible week when the war swept across it, but on this bright day, with a sky full of big cumulus clouds which sometimes hid the sun but never brought rain, I noticed how fast the work of reconstruction was progressing. The farms and their barns still looked shabby but many fewer showed the clear evidence of shell or bomb I'd seen only a month before.

On the outskirts of the town a police inspector mounted the bus. Slowly he moved down the aisle towards me. Though my well-forged papers should be proof against a casual inspection, I sat forward in my seat, soaked in sweat, my jacket hanging loose so a quick reach behind my tie through my open shirt buttons would bring my hand to the Luger's butt. At the same time I checked the instructions for opening the bus's emergency door which I'd chosen to sit by. Raising my eyes from these, I saw on the pavement beside the stopped bus, a row of three more inspectors.

There they stood, motionless, greatcoated, waiting. I couldn't see their faces, just the tops of their uniform caps. I found those three faceless figures even more alarming then the inspector inside the bus.

He came towards me with agonising slowness, first staring at each person's papers then taking a careful look at his face as if checking him against some identikit memory. When he did the same to me I went on casually looking down at a newspaper on the seat beside me — but the sudden snap of his punch on my ticket started my hand with a convulsive jerk towards my shirt buttons. I diverted it to my breast-pocket handkerchief and contrived a sneeze.

That search encouraged me. Things were less under control than they pretended. It also alerted me. When I left the bus I moved *away* from the centre of town, stopping occasionally to look into shop windows and check behind me.

I noticed again that there were fewer true shortages than I'd expected but that the goods had become grotesquely shoddy so they took less and less manufacturing effort, and their prices had risen so that fewer and fewer people could afford them. It's the same with food: there's enough if you have the money and it's packaged with the traditional labels, but it's flabby, amorphous, as if all made from the same cabbage-stalk cellulose blended with different chemical flavourings. As for the bread, the second it's moistened it collapses into a substance like soggy tissue paper.

Satisfied that I was alone, I came by a big circuit to Durville's central square. It contained two cafés, each with big spreads of tables below canvas awnings; I had no doubt which I wanted. Standing directly opposite it, watching those pavement tables, I could rest my back against the grey granite blocks of the town police station.

54

Suddenly — I never saw him come — a tall heavy man was sitting there ordering coffee. Though this strange person had carroty hair and a carroty, drooping moustache, M.S.G.'s big Roman nose was unmistakable.

I sat at his table and ordered coffee. I made casual remarks about the day's newspaper stories and today's lousy instant coffee substitute. 'It's been a hard winter' — before I'd half said it I realised that this password had been designed for last month and the past four weeks of summer weather must make it a glaring oddity. Since the blowing of Detergent it might anyway have been changed.

He detected the tiny hesitation in my voice. Watching me, he gave no answer.

What could I do to prove my genuineness? Show him my gun? Tell him in plain language, our own language, who I was? Mention mutual friends in Ops? There seemed nothing which would for certain distinguish me from a counter-agent supplied with the facts by the confession of a captured member of our circuit. This grotesque situation continued for half an hour. There we sat facing each other, both in serious need of each other's help, but with no way to ask for it.

Three more Sundays I sat with M.S.G., drinking coffee, exchanging small talk about prices and weather (to explain my bus trips to the Patrases I invented an aunt in Durville — my mother's sister in case they checked the local phone book). We seemed locked in some astonishing battle of wills, though exactly how to define this battle I still don't know.

He never made the smallest facial gesture which would show that we were anything more than café acquaintances. I took my tone from his. I approved. In training we'd been told the story of the newly arrived agent who was taken to a restaurant where he found his complete circuit enjoying an excellent meal, telling loud officers'- mess stories in their own language. That agent was so shocked he cut off all contact with them and the best evidence for his story was that none of them were around to deny it. My conflict with M.S.G. seemed also connected with security, almost it seemed with which of us would break down and confess first. I began to know that I was losing.

The fourth time we met he said unexpectedly, 'Like to drop by? Take a snifter?'

It was the invitation I'd longed for. Casually I nodded — only to find that he hadn't meant now but on some future Sunday perhaps. I sensed that merely by accepting I'd somehow lost another round.

I went a fifth Sunday. As always I approached circuitously and lingered beside those great granite blocks of Durville police station to check the forecourt tables. There he sat, big and hunched, his carroty hair and droopy moustache suggesting the pathetic attempts of some shabby middle-aged person to be young and debonair. About to cross and sit with him, I saw two other men take the vacant chairs at his table.

Members of his circuit? Casual acquaintances from work? I changed direction and circled the square.

By the time I returned all three of them were talking with surprising intensity. My conversations with M.S.G. had been more casual: I'd speak towards the passing traffic, he'd answer into his paper. I set off to circle the square again, but hadn't gone five paces before, glancing back, I saw them all three rise, cross the street and get into a car which now slid out of a turning where it had been hidden. A hospital car.

From the moment I recognised that car I held my breath expecting a sudden scuffle, a shot, running feet, a body on the pavement. Instead he went without a struggle. They even made little bows to each other as they let him in first then sat one on either side of him . . .

By good luck the Hospital for Social Diseases which serves the province is in this town, though it stands in a suburb which I'd never visited. We went at four in the afternoon when my shift ended, bicycling together through the main gates. Here Lena showed her out-patient's pass and mine which she'd got by telling her psychologist of a friend who wanted to become a hospital visitor.

Beyond the gates we entered a long drive between ten-metre-high banks of rhododendrons. Before the town expanded this must have been a prosperous country estate. Among those vast bushes we began to see figures. Some stood still, resting on their sticks, staring at us with the grey perception of lunatics which throws such disturbing doubt on the bright clear way *we* see the world. Others lay asleep on wooden seats, their mouths open, wrapped in overcoats despite the hot sun. Still others lurked at the edges of ornamental lawns, but five seconds later — when I had the cycle under control again — had disappeared leaving only an impression of eyes watching from the shadows of dark shrubs. A powerful stench of azalea hung over the whole drive and its bordering lawns.

Among these grey creatures I searched for M.S.G. and for that other thin young face. At the same time I felt horror in case I found them and instead of human recognition saw blank eyes staring from minds which had been already destroyed. Indeed, what really horrified me about all these poor lunatics was that every one of them must have been a potential resistance worker. Put away here by relations who they'd frightened by some minor failure to conform, they'd been reduced to cabbages. No wonder so few of them seemed to expect visitors.

After several hundred metres we came in sight of a red brick façade with pre-First-War pillarettes around its windows and the non-structural relief of a romanesque arch above its door. On all sides attached by walk-ways with corrugated plastic roofs were the pre-fabricated huts of extra wards, canteens, laundries and shops. Grouped round the main building, they suggested the direction our civilisation is taking, from tall mansion to burrow-like hut. Above one rose a brick crematorium chimney.

At the entrance to her out-patients hut we parted. She was to wait here in her psychologist's ante-room. She was nervous but it seemed the best plan. If anyone questioned her she'd discover with surprise that she'd got the date of her appointment wrong, cycle away and meet me halfway down the drive. If not, I'd come back for her in an hour.

Meanwhile, mixing with arriving visitors, I entered the central building by its main door and at once adopted another role: inmate taking exercise. Relaxing the muscles of my left leg so that it dragged after me like a limp flipper, I began to move in a slow purposeless way, as if the longer it took me the more minutes of the day I'd kill. Spasmodically I screwed one side of my face into an expression of gripping internal conflict. That corridor of green plastic tiles decorated with the framed daubs of occupational therapy classes and reeking of ether made my act easy. Ether has always nauseated me.

Noting the name of the first ward — Beauchamp — I turned into the second — Villeneuve — and became again a visitor. I walked confidently into its outer room and sat

58

in a low utility armchair as if waiting for a patient to shamble out from the opaque glass doors of the ward itself, fragments of cabbage soup hanging from his lips. If questioned I'd discover with surprise that I was in Villeneuve when I wanted Beauchamp.

At once someone sat next to me. He wore a grey hospital gown and was distressingly emaciated. His chin, covered with white stubble, was joined to his neck by two cork-like tendons covered with wrinkled grey skin. In a low insistent way, leaning close so that I could smell the paraldehyde on his breath, he began to tell me how badly they were treated here.

'You make one tiny mistake, you're for it.'

'For it?'

Widening his eyes in a parody of horror, he put a curled finger to each temple: the places where they fit the terminals for Electro-Convulsive Therapy. Gripping my knee with bony fingers he went on staring continuously and almost unblinkingly at me. His stare seemed a challenge. Of course you don't believe me, how could you, he seemed to be saying.

'Listen,' I began in a low whisper. My mouth still open, wondering how to continue, I was distracted by another patient passing close in front of me across the room's floor, shuffling himself backwards on his buttocks. He'd no sooner gone than a younger one, also in grey dressing-gown, arrived carrying a chair. He placed this a metre into the room, sat in it and began to stare at the old man beside me with intense hate. 'Miserable old sod.'

'Be quiet,' the old man said.

'Incontinent.'

'Don't listen to him,' the old man said.

'They took his bed pan away,' the young man said, still

59

looking at the old one, though now apparently speaking to me. 'That's what it's all about.'

The old man began to cry.

To escape from this scene in which by ill luck I'd become involved, I crossed to another chair, dodging on my way two white-coated male nurses carrying the patient who'd recently passed on his buttocks. Because they carried him back the way he'd come in exactly the same sitting position he suggested a mechanical toy being restarted on a track.

Too far off now to hear what that other pair were saying, I sensed that they were still locked in an act of sadistic bullying. The technique of the place, I realised, was to reduce the inmates to animals who snarled and squabbled together thus destroying their chances of ever regaining self-respect. I also sensed, especially from that awful buttock-scraping crossing of the room, so unnecessarily close in front of my chair, an appeal to me as an outsider, an inarticulate cry for pity, understanding and help. For readmission on *any* terms to the world they'd been excluded from.

'I don't believe we've had the pleasure . . .'

Another was standing in front of me. Wearing a dark blue suit with bright blue tie, cleanly shaven with brushed hair, there was nothing odd about him except his formal position, feet together, head slightly bowed, hand held out.

'Klinger's the name. They probably told you. Been here long?'

So this was the new way inmates arrived. Suddenly I guessed it. No alarming arrest of formal certification. Just a voluntary surrender when their guilt became unbearable.

'No, no . . .' I began and realised I'd spoken far too loudly. All around the room many were staring at me, others glancing towards the staff entrance from which a male nurse must soon emerge with loaded syringe. They not only knew the form but, far more disgusting, were getting pleasure from the fact that this time it was happening to someone else. The smartly suited one opposite me showed least surprise. Like an actor who knows that to laugh himself will kill his joke, he went on holding out his hand for me to shake. When I rose and hurried out his eyes followed me with an actor's deadpan disbelief.

A strange thing happened when I went to fetch Lena from her psychologist's hut. To my surprise, still some distance away, I saw her standing half-in half-out of its door, holding this open with her arse, as if waiting for me.

I came towards her less and less quickly. Now I saw that she was beckoning me, as if inviting me in. Ten paces from her I came to a complete halt.

'What is it?'

She didn't answer but still beckoned.

'Is he there?' Had the crazy girl mentioned me to him so that he now wanted to consult me about her case?

She just went on beckoning.

'Come on,' I said sharply and turned away towards the bicycle park. Presently I heard her running feet behind me.

'What was that all about?'

She shook her head abstractedly. 'Look,' she called, pointing ahead. We both looked but there was nothing to look at.

I became sterner, but at once she began to stare at me in that big-eyed, scared way which told me that even if I made her answer it would mean nothing.

The simplest explanation is probably the best. The way she'd been able to arrange our visit made her so happy she wanted to show me every angle of it, hoping for more praise.

7

AT the factory there's a labour relations officer. I was taken to him with other new workers soon after I arrived. It's because of Harris, the L.R.O., that I've again postponed our operation.

I call him Harris because he resembles my mother's fishmonger in the seaside town where I was born. True, that Harris wore a boater, but below it there was this same long melancholy face. To amuse me when I was about six Harris the fishmonger would lift his boater and show his nearly bald head, ill-covered by sweaty wisps of black hair. I'd grip my mother's hand and press my face into her skirt above her knee — that was how tall I was. Harris the labour relations officer also has a bald patch, ill-covered by lank black hair.

Another of that fishmonger's tricks was to shake hands with trusting children. Shyly I remember reaching up for his big red hand the first time it happened — and finding hidden in his palm a cold wet sprat. This trick must have produced a more sensational effect on me than on previous victims because whenever he saw me coming he'd make as if to repeat it while his two assistants would stop work and prepare to fall about with delight. The worst feature of this pantomime was the way my mother seemed unaware of it. She'd be ordering halibut when, without ever taking his eyes off her, Harris would jerk his big water-sodden hand towards me, making me flinch away. 'Stop fidgeting, Brian,' my mother would say. 'And two nice big juicy cods' heads for the cats please, Mr. Harris.' Though she must have been dimly aware of our special relationship because, distressingly, she would always call him, 'Your friend Mr. Harris.'

Harris, our L.R.O., is the person who most alarms me. In fact he's the only one who seems to notice me at all. The others go about with their eyes down. Of course Harris notices me, I reassure myself; he notices everyone, it's his job, a technique he's been taught. But that's hardly reassuring because the purpose of his watching technique is to see which of us it causes to disintegrate. Surely he can see how recently learned my bench skills are. If I lift my eyes to his I believe they may instantly — out of my control — confess all to him.

I can even tell that Harris has come into the machine shop and begun to watch me before I've seen him. Suddenly my brain locks with alarm. No doubt I've detected similar tension in all around me.

But occasionally I get an idea which is almost more alarming: that he may be one of us; that he's testing my discretion, waiting for the moment when he can trust me. I know that I must treat this as some desperate wish-fulfilment dream, even if I later discover it's true.

The incident I needed to clarify began three days ago as soon as I'd passed the punch clock on my way in. A voice, close but from someone I couldn't see, said, 'Morning, Meyer.'

In that factory, which is anyway so loud with machinery it's hard to speak to another person, I've believed I'm anonymous, more thing than person, part of the machine I operate. I was shocked to discover that someone knew my name, more to see a second later that it was

Harris. There he stood close beyond the clocks watching the morning shift filter past. I gave a start not unlike those convulsive jerks I used to give away from that fishmonger's big red fist.

Glancing back I saw Harris occasionally speaking to others as they passed, playing the good L.R.O. — or perhaps proving to me that I hadn't been an exception.

The morning coffee break came. Emerging from the subterranean passage to the canteen I saw Harris again. With still more ostentatious democracy, he was in the queue itself, ten ahead of me by the time I reached it.

Now I saw Lena too, half hidden by self-service sandwich cases, wearing her white linen canteen cap, pouring coffee substitute infusion from a giant metal pot, moving the flow up and down the rows of cups like a hose. Surreptitiously I watched her, noticing the way she blushed dark red and stared at anyone who jollied her. It's always the same ones who do. Put them in front of a canteen girl and as predictably as a machine they'll make an obscene suggestion.

At the second Harris came opposite Lena the man in front of me in the queue reched back past me for the pat of margarine substitute he'd missed, blocking my view. It was Lena's idiot stare which told me that Harris had also made an obscene suggestion to her.

Others I didn't mind — they were no more offensive than dogs who can't help sniffing the private parts of any bitch they pass. Harris was too intelligent to be excused in this way. By using Lena as a creature in his plan to democratise himself he truly insulted her, and she knew it. White-faced instead of red, her eyes kept straying to his back view moving away across the canteen, so that by the time I reached her, her tray of cups was awash with brown fluid.

I took mine and moved on without a glance at her.

That evening she'd only been in my room for a couple of minutes when she said, 'Got a new boy friend.' Kneeling on the floor she watched me where I sat, as if to be sure I understood.

'Who's that?' When Lena's aroused her breath has a bitter smell. To my surprise during our quick kiss I'd already detected it.

'Your friend Mr. Harris.'

Though I remembered planning to tell her about Harris, for a disturbing instant I couldn't recall actually doing it. Slowly it came back. We'd agreed, I even remembered, to codename him after my childhood fishmonger. Odd that she should use my mother's exact phrase, but perhaps I'd mentioned that too.

'He dated me.'

I talked seriously to Lena about security.

' "Like a night out, ducks?" he says. Dirty old man.'

I told her it could be the break in our luck I'd long hoped for, but more probably meant we were both suspect. Now that the time for action was close . . .

She looked at me with wide excited eyes. Her lips — which are thick like a trumpet player's — came apart as if she wanted but didn't dare ask me to say it again.

'Notice his questions. Notice the subjects he starts.'

The day of her date was the hottest yet. Summer is reaching its height. Work in that windowless factory full of howling machines has become hellish. The evenings when the racket of the afternoon's snarled-up fuming traffic has died are calm and beautiful. I sit up here above the town, my window wide, listening to voices starting in the street below as it becomes cool enough for people to think again. They talk quietly and sometimes laugh.

Suddenly I'm hopeful. Even in this town where the war effort occupies everyone's time six days a week and propaganda-induced fears and greeds most of the rest, whenever the enemy isn't watching something better from long ago starts to happen. I love those people down below me who have come quietly on to their doorsteps and are finding time to talk to each other, or just to notice each other, which they've ceased to do by day.

A moment later I'm bitterly angry with them. These weak passive conversations are the sum of their protest, when they should be screaming with outraged anger. 'Do not go quiet . . .' the words of the poet come to me. In order to survive, they would argue, they must conform, then one day they will perhaps be bolder — dead they can never be. It *isn't* survival, I want to shout at them. By pretending to feel no anger they cease to *be* angry. Their every action and thought should be informed with bitter resentment of their condition and of the enemy who enforces it, *now* before it's too late.

By now Jane will have received almost half the cards I left for Ops despatch unit to post her one a week, with West Country postmarks, telling her that my training continues uneventfully — assuming they've gone on sending them although they believe I'm dead or captured. Perhaps I've set them a problem: how long to send cards from the dead. Has Jane begun to notice that my cards never answer hers?

Jane is married — the postcards go care of her hairdresser. She even laughed when I told her that, not as if she found it funny but as if such a parody must prove that the whole story of my new job and imminent departure was an elaborate tease . . .

Hubby we called him. She used to tell me about Hubby's waistcoat, and gold watchchain, and single false tooth — result of a tumble from his prep-school wooden horse — on its pink plastic plate, grotesquely distorted in its night-time glass of water. For my sake she probably exaggerated the repulsion these things caused her but I liked to hear them.

Because of Hubby we met at lunch-times — like me he was protected from the call-up; at twenty-seven his heart has a whisper — and made love in the beds of servicemen's clubs to which we bribed our way, only occasionally escaping from wartime weekends at forlorn seaside resorts. There we'd walk the windy promenades, our love for each other enhanced by these ghost towns, thinking of the pre-war bank holiday crowds which are such a well-established national memory that we seemed almost to be visiting historical sites — though my private memory sometimes suggested that those bone-freezing places had always had a run-down, where-is-everyone-*this*-year, whatever-can-we-do-now flavour. But I never said so to Jane because she wouldn't have wanted to know. Put two people together and they start to lie, even if they love each other — because they love each other.

Still less could I have mentioned the moments of flatness during those weekends, which really did glow then and do even more now, moments at which I missed the excitement of our secret lunch-time pub assignations when at any moment we might meet one of Hubby's friends and when his presence in his near-by chambers was a constant aphrodisiac.

Jane, Jane — she was perhaps six years older than Lena but so much more a child. Though I believed in her unhappy marriage I would have liked her to put into words this conclusion, which her descriptions of her physically repulsive legal husband surely led to. Once, looking out of my office window — she'd just dropped by to tell me how

67

distractedly she loved me, in case I'd misunderstood her phone call of half an hour before — I saw them far down the street, where she perhaps believed they were out of sight, waiting together for a cab. What impressed me was how steadily she stared at that black-suited, stout little man, an umbrella dangling from his wooden arm, and how close their faces were together. Not love, I never suspected that. Probably hate, but a disturbingly intimate hate I'd rather not have known about.

I made no scene, I had no reason. Scenes anyway belonged to another sort of affair. It was unthinkable to say or do anything which would make Jane unhappy. Was that why I never suggested she left him? Or did I enjoy the sense that despite the way she seemed to despise him some part of her was tied to him in a way I couldn't break and wouldn't even understand? Did I like my status in that affair of small boy desiring a relationship he wasn't adult enough to have?

I made her unhappy in the end. Incredulous is a better word. 'But you don't have to.' She said it again and again, about my to-her insane decision.

I think she only went on seeing me because part of her believed to the end that I'd suddenly laugh and tell her it was all a joke. I'd catch her staring at me in untypical silence. She'd give a little angry dismissive shake of her head. It just couldn't be true. That I, safe in a reserved job . . . no, no, impossible.

I was only irritated with her when I hesitated. They were pressing me to stay. I was passed from flattering desk to flattering desk, each grey-haired incumbent more informal producing better sherry in finer-cut glass. 'You have a small but rare skill.'

I could use that in my new job, I argued, referring to my languages, a genetic legacy from my White Russian father I never met, but in fact they were meaning something harder to describe, part cunning, part empathy, which made me a strangely successful interrogator of political refugees ...

Am I being disloyal to Jane? I have no desire to press complicated truth into any such easily handled package. Certainly I loved her. Now I love Lena and think less of Jane. To attach pasts or futures to these truths is misleading and pointless.

The package I'd just handed myself, I realised with a shock, was that I loved Lena. At the same moment I heard noises in the house below, running steps on the stairs, no children's counting games tonight, a knock at my door ...

She'd let him take her home then slipped out again, a risk but I was too glad to see her to criticise.

'What happened?'

'The brush-off,' she said, and mimed a still drooling but drooping Harris, making him look like a sad labrador, as I realise he always has.

A little angrily I told her she'd missed a chance. I saw terror on her face. It began to go out of shape. She'd arrived expecting praise for what she'd done. If I said one more stern thing she'd scream. The new confidence I'd given her was more fragile than I'd realised.

We made love. We lay close together, gasping and raising our eyebrows at the pleasure we gave each other and our skilful timing. Despite this I felt there was something missing and was puzzled. Presently she moved her face away as if to watch me.

She was hoping that at last I might tell her I'd fixed a date.

'Any day now.'

8

THE low tent-shaped ceiling of this room presses down on me. Like the walls, it's pale green.

Down the passage outside feet pass continuously. They come closer — bent over my transmitting key or with my mouth innocently full of toothbrush, I grow rigid watching my glossy green door. They pass by. Any pair could belong to a Visiting corporal or sergeant — it's not an officers' hotel.

Perhaps I'm safer here, under their noses, on M.S.G.'s principle. It didn't save him.

Not that they wear uniform — another change since my training. You rarely see those glossy black patent-leather caps, or shining high boots I've hated since I was a child. It's part of a plan to make the occupation less offensive.

But they remain easy to recognise by their issue civilian clothes which go so improbably with their square jaws and cruel, brainwashed eyes. Greed stares out of every pair — and terror too, that someone may tempt them to think something forbidden. They wear their hair fashionably long, but not so long they'd scare themselves, they mispronounce vowels when they talk the local language, oh I can recognise them all right. Though I keep my real hate for the collaborators. I see so many I suspect the whole running of this sad country will soon be in their hands. How harmless they seem. A few have ostentatious modern cars in fashionable rust-red or French mustard shades, but most are gentle, considerate people, hard to dislike. 'I don't want to trouble you,' they say. 'Sorry to be a bother.'

How disgusting! To accept their living deaths. To put moral pressure on others to live this death with them. 'Sorry *not* to be a bother,' would be better. 'Sorry for ever saying anything so killingly boring it *doesn't* trouble you' . . .

It began two days ago. As usual I stopped work at four and came home on foot, through streets thick with engine fumes which the fierce sun turned opaque, among the jostling, down-looking citizens of Urbville. To them it was a day no different from any other of their long captivity. To me it was more important. That evening I would give Lena a final briefing. As soon as I entered my room I saw that everything had been moved.

Not dramatically but unmistakably. As if they'd been picked up, examined and put down carefully again, but not carefully enough. I couldn't attach my feeling to any particular object — that day I'd set no traps — only to a general conviction my whole room gave me. It wasn't how I'd left it.

Certain though I was, I wanted Lena to confirm it, but she wasn't due for three hours. I wonder who has tried to live in a room for three hours without touching anything.

For half an hour it was a moment by moment struggle. A change occurred. Sitting by my chair my body grew quieter, became slightly numb, but my mind went hurrying faster. Below in the street — it was becoming another evening of cool relief after that mind-devastating afternoon — someone had locked up a cat on heat. Its howls were police sirens. Then they were the howls of political prisoners who knew their heads were about to be put into machines. Presently the only physical sensation left me was the feel of the lump made by that tiny pill below the lapel of my jacket. Pressing against my collar bone, it seemed to grow enormous.

At last she came. On a normal evening she might at once have stood close to me, letting me smell and touch her, asking me quickly, quickly to undress and love her. Naked, she might have kept me waiting by some crazy love-flight into a dark corner of the room where she'd have crouched, pretending to weep and begging me for mercy with such genuine persistent despair she'd have half convinced me. That night my anxious question stopped her. Still dressed, she began to go round the room acting idiot Visiting Policeman, picking up things, smelling them, staring at them held close to the end of her nose then at arm's length, making imaginary notes on her cuff, getting on to her hands and knees to sniff the bed legs.

It distressed me. Once I'd loved these acts, the early stages of the slow process of making her a sane adult again. Now they seemed a regression. I'd let the security I'd given her seem frail by showing my own alarm. At any moment she might retreat again behind the front of idiot-child she'd used for the three years before I came.

Telling her to wait, I hurried to the ground floor, reaching it just as young Patras came out of their living-room — a fine misnomer.

'Did I have a Visitor today?' That pun wasn't an accident. I watched him for its effect.

'Haven't you got one now?'

'That's not what I mean' — so all these months he'd been checking me.

'What *do* you mean then?'

I began to shout at him. 'My room's private. Is that understood? Why do you imagine I came here?'

The noise I was making terrified him. He took a pace

72

forward as if to strike me. When I moved quickly back he began to mouth silent words, his fury screwing up and distorting his big soft face, showing the bully behind the slob.

Their living-room door reopened and Mrs. Patras came out.

'Says he's not satisfied with his room,' young Patras said.

'Dissatisfied with his room, is he?' Mrs. Patras said. At once they set up a priest and response ritual.

'Some people don't know when they're lucky.'

'Give 'em the earth, they're still not happy.'

'Reckon he'd better find somewhere else.'

'Not before he pays for all that extra laundry.'

About to reply, it stopped me dead. What extra laundry?

'Him and his filthy ways.'

'Whose house does he think this is?'

Groping for some sense — or code — in their words, I glanced sideways through the door she'd left open and saw grandfather Patras laughing so much he'd set himself choking. His face deep purple, one hand at his throat, he swayed about but couldn't stop himself. At his side his free hand made convulsive motions almost as if he was encouraging his dog to run out and snap at their heels.

By the time my attention returned to them they'd turned and were going back down their passage. They passed through their door and shut it. Astonished, I wondered if they'd said some final thing I'd missed. What were they going to do?

Now wasn't the moment to ask. Packing, I imagined his flabby hands — he wore a tiny embedded ruby on one little finger — lifting and examining every one of my private possessions. Photographing them, perhaps. All the time I listened for the faint ring of the telephone coming off its rest in the house below.

Quarter of an hour later as we came downstairs each carrying one weighty case there was continuous talking from behind their closed door, as if they were all speaking and none of them listening, suggesting a disturbed nest of bees. It was too confused to catch any words and I didn't stop to try.

We sat together at a café, keeping the cases between our knees, waiting for the evening to darken into night. Again I had the impression that I was hearing the distant and distinctive hum of our bombers. I tried to catch Lena's eye to ask without words whether she could hear it too. Worried and thoughtful, she sat looking at one of her hands where it lay on the cream plastic table top. Sometimes she gave its thumb a tiny twitch, as if to make sure it was hers.

Suddenly from only a few streets away came the howls of a band of Youth League. We had let it grow dangerously late, almost curfew — though the exact hour of this is less certain since the hooter has been discontinued. Instead, looking round in the early night, you realise that streets which were busy a few moments ago are emptying fast, some people actually running. Lugging our heavy but fragile cases which banged alarmingly against our legs we also ran. We were lucky. We met no patrols or marauding bands. I left her with them at the door of her hostel and hurried on.

Soon I was moving across that big construction site near the station, subject of several of my early radio reports. Running and ducking in the moonlight, bright here away from enclosing streets, I reached a group of large concrete pipes. I dodged into the nearest of these, crawled to its far end which was blocked by an earth bank and settled myself for a long stay.

After many painful hours on that hard curve of concrete I did at last sleep better than I'd intended, and woke to see, past my shoes, that my pipe's entrance was a bright white circle, as if day had come long ago. Not especially worried — dawn is early in summer, safer here than wandering conspicuously about a deserted town — I glanced at my watch: 7.40. Only twenty minutes till my shift. Hurriedly I attempted to reverse myself, decided my pipe was too narrow and began to crawl out feet first.

At once a noise stopped me. Faint at first, it came rapidly closer. Long before I was prepared for it, my bright circle of light turned black and that whooping cry was howled directly in at me. Certain I was discovered, I crouched there, waiting to be called out, but now, astonishingly, my exit was bright again and I heard near-by pipes echoing to the same Red-Indian howls. A morning sport of children on their way to school? I smiled, though my ears still sang.

He came back. Now he seemed actually to peer in as he howled. I clutched my gun which in my alarm I'd half drawn, though I doubted if I could use it: in this concrete tube it might burst my ears, and anyway how could I shoot an innocent schoolboy. Again my exit cleared but now, sickening, I remembered it was Saturday and there'd be no school.

All morning they howled in at me. For half an hour there'd be peace then the pounding of small feet across gravel would be followed by sudden darkness and a hideous yell. Each time the sound stayed echoing round my pipe for many seconds.

Presently I realised that work had begun on the site. Heavy machinery roared and the ground vibrated. Sometimes a vast yellow earth-mover, its tyres as tall as a man, came grinding close past, sometimes one appeared far off climbing a slope of raw clay. Suppose today was pipe-laying day. I imagined my pipe rising . . .

I tried to be amused at the surprise my friends in Ops would get if they saw me crouching here, terrorised by the local high-school Redskins. Would Judd be amused? How would he view my recent actions? Individually I could justify each of them, but the total result might seem deplorable.

About midday several of those schoolboys came and sat on my pipe, yelling defiance from here at their mates. This pipe was their stockade. It occurred to one of them to beat defiantly on its side with his metal heeled shoes. The rest imitated him. I blocked my ears.

I slipped out during the siesta. In dazzling sunshine the site was sinisterly quiet. The halted machines were parked in a group near a huge orange crater they're making — whatever for? A few drivers sitting in their shade were eating from paper bags.

Today Lena and I found this second-class hotel. It has one advantage. It's close to my factory. Looking for the first time from its window, I found myself staring from a mere hundred metres at that disproportionately large administrative wing, the central objective of my mission. At least I am now perfectly placed to make detailed observations from the outside . . . It's like a piece of good luck I *might once* have had.

Sitting here waiting for Lena, I'm not allowing myself to look into a certain dark corner. I force myself to look to prove there's nothing there. Moving softly — I suddenly open that glossy green door to the corridor. Empty. My nerves are on edge. Isolation. I need a break. For me there can be no break yet.

The green colour of this room reminds me of another. My last at home. It's almost as if that elegant bachelor's room with its view on to a leafy corner of The Hospital's grounds, has been subjected to instant ageing. I can imagine trick photography making its paint peel, its carpet grow holes, its wardrobe curtain sag all in a few seconds.

Jane only came there once — the day before I left. I was in uniform — she'd never seen that either. She kept staring from me in khaki and Sam Brown — more joke? — to its neatly made bed and tidy dust-free surfaces.

'Is this where you live?'

'Anything wrong?' It had a Jacobean oak chest and sideboard which made a pair. Beyond The Hospital grounds it looked away to distant bridges and cranes, then to still more distant cloud banks over the tidelands of the estuary. In winter I would stare hopelessly down that corridor of escape, in summer impatiently.

'You always lived here?'

It was as if my room made me a different person and she wasn't sure she approved.

'Why not?'

'Come on.' We spent the afternoon looking for a present she could buy me. All the time she was giving me new glances of appraisal. Because I hadn't realised we were going on such a prolonged search I lost the chance of suggesting we first made love in my bed. As a result we never did.

In this shabby version of my smart Chelsea room there's a basin with taps but the hot doesn't run and the cold only produces an orange trickle. Now that I've been sitting still for half an hour a cockroach is exploring this basin. He pauses on its rim, seeing me with surprise, wondering whether I'm alive. Uncertain, he dips quickly over the rim into the crater of the basin, but he's not so clever as he thinks because he's left a tiny something showing. Foot? Eye? I suspect he's watching me, thinking he can't be seen . . .

I've just crushed him with the heel of my slipper and forced his little smelly corpse past the metal cross piece down the basin's drain. The moment before I struck his eye seemed to look up and catch mine . . .

It's coded Double Y, I shall tell Lena, from the shape of its two gigantic support pillars. It's one of many subsidiary targets most of which we were instructed to set aside till that great night, even of the Second Coming, when the network we had created would blow fifty bridges, when a thousand separate acts of sabotage all over occupied territory would cripple the enemy's troop movements. Imagining myself explaining this to Lena I see more vividly than ever the contrast between the pair of us operating here in lonely isolation and that optimistic fantasy Ops helped us cultivate. Then, because our attention was concentrated on our agents, it seemed that they, not the local population, were this country's principal feature. If I were ever lonely I could drop into the kitchen of *any* café and stand a good chance of finding an active cell . . .

I shall describe to Lena the pre-war photos of Double Y we were shown, and how, because it was my particular scheme, I visited an old foreman who'd been employed on its construction . . .

The bridge-builder showed me one he hadn't sent to Ops — in answer to the national appeal for such photos. In it he was sitting on the base of one of the twin pillars with a girl — a workmate must have snapped him. Though his face was turned towards her and he was trying to keep his arm round her back, she was leaning

78

away, not facing him, but her mouth was open. She was probably telling him not to be saucy. That picture held a foretaste of their next forty years together — and he didn't see it. The person I really hated, of course, was her mother. Odd how I remember that picture better than all those important facts he told me about boreholes, girders and tracks . . .

The scene set, I shall describe to Lena the vital help she must give me when we reach that pool of floodlight where the twin tracks leave solid ground for the suspended steel girders of Double Y. I can imagine her excitement — touched with disbelief that it's really about to happen.

Later we'll make love with the blankets over our heads, as we sometimes do, in a dark cocoon.

Part Two

I

ANNYA is coming tonight.

She's short, with black hair, which falls below her shoulder blades when she lets it out of her day-time secretary's knot — and freckles. Black hair and freckles — a strange mixture. She doesn't at all resemble ... She's almost the exact opposite of ..

Any minute now I'll hear her running steps on the stairs — no resident non-commissioned officer comes up stairs the way Annya does. Her running doesn't vary from flight to flight, as if she's acting one part from ground floor to first, another from first to second ... She comes up straight and fast and busy. Anyone who didn't know would take her for a sensible efficient, well-adjusted girl.

Only now, when I've known Annya for a month can I bear to remember what happened.

For more than a month I've lived from day to day, solving immediate problems, refusing to think ahead or back. I've reduced it to 'something', with no more detail than a heap covered by a sheet. And even this I've seen only out of the corner of my eye in case if I looked directly at it I might start to remember what was below and begin to cry out, as I seemed to be doing for days afterwards, Take me away, I'm not fit for this work, you should never have sent me.

I've found myself standing still in the street or in some part of my room, unsure where I was going or what I was about to do, saying over and over to myself, Oh no, oh surely not.

If I've thought at all this last month I've thought how easy it would be to give up, not become an active traitor, simply cease to operate. My disguise has lasted since spring. Perhaps it could last indefinitely. I could lead a comfortable, not unhappy, fairly safe life. And I'd be justified. Bewhiskered Judd, his safe mustachioed dummies with their barks of simulated jingoism — they had no right to test me so severely. Discovering something so different from anything they'd warned me to expect, I'm entitled to cancel my contract. If I ever got back I'd defend my actions. Whenever I've had such thoughts before I've grown angry. Crazy lunatic, observe the facts, how could you sink into this mass of accepting people, this brainwashed mire of pathetic creatures? Why not? I've been wondering.

My work at the factory, the thing I might have been most anxious to abandon, has helped. I can go on doing it without decision or responsibility. Ironically, it has drawn me back to my proper work. My hands and arms which move those brakes and levers so automatically hour after hour, have once again seemed to grow separate from me and my freed mind has begun to think and think. Separated from my physical self, I've recovered the sense I

82

used to get of enormous grasp and power, of an intelligence which can watch and hear and understand and plan. I've known again that the time will come when I can leave this quiet but infinitely strong position and begin to operate . . .

The night I'd chosen wasn't the night I'd told Lena. It was the night before. But she was coming to see me for what I'd called a last reconnaissance. It was an elementary precaution. Do I wish I hadn't taken it?

As soon as she arrived, just after darkness had settled on the town, I told her the plan had been put forward twenty-four hours. Though I watched her carefully and saw her intense excitement I seemed no longer able to guess its cause. Shock? Or merely the brink of action?

Bandoliers of gelignite, percussion detonators, wrench — borrowed from my factory tool kit — unarmed-combat wire, torch, burnt cork. We checked my list, wound the bandoliers round our stomachs and hid the rest in pockets. All the time Lena kept stopping to stare at me, as if the fact that we were truly about to go was hitting her in waves.

From the hotel's back door we crunched across its garden, littered with old cans and smelling of frying potatoes. The full moon hidden above thickish cloud, the night was neither bright nor black, excellent for our purpose. We climbed a low wall and reached a narrow service road.

Near the edge of town we passed a public phone box. I must reconnoitre ahead, I told her. She must wait for me. Keeping close to the house fronts, I moved forward quickly and softly and turned abruptly down a side street out of her view.

I gave her thirty seconds. I remember deciding not to give her more and thus test her too hard — how illogical that seems. I returned running quickly. Not only was her hand on the door of the phone box, but because I was running silently in my sock-covered shoes and she hadn't yet heard me, she actually went on opening it. I was only five paces away when at last she heard me.

Her whole body jolted. She was so shocked it was several seconds before she could turn fully away from that phone box and face me.

We went on out of town, across field and heath. I hope never again to live through such hours. It was as if we were moving forward together only because we had no idea what else to do. What had happened had set us a problem too big for us.

In a gravelled lane she came close to me and whispered, 'If they'd come, what would I have told them?'

Crouching in a ditch, carefully blacking each other's hands and faces, she said, 'They let you make emergency calls.'

How soft her face was under the pressure of the cork. When I pressed on the black skin it drew up her lip, momentarily showing her white teeth. In her black face her thick trumpet-player's lips were negroid.

'Suppose you hadn't come back,' she said.

I gave her the cork. It was her turn to black mine.

Her swift unexplained meeting with the man in the dark overcoat the night I followed her. That date with Harris, so quickly confessed because I'd seen him make it, such a non-event later. The way she'd stood at the door of her psychologist's hut, beckoning me in . . . The way, naked, she pressed herself to me, asking to be loved. I could make no sense of it. I see us drifting forward together — till it was too late. I suppose I still hoped for a miracle. The persuasive arguments have all come later: to postpone it would have given her a whole day to warn them. Now that she knew that I knew I couldn't even dismiss her and attempt it alone.

Across open fields, grey under the clouded moon, along the black fringes of woods and spinneys, I never let her get more than a few paces from me. I believe she realised and accepted it, almost found it proper.

Our final approach was along a ditch still muddy with a trickle of water despite the hot summer. She was to climb from this while I stayed crouching. Standing just out of the light from his signal box and from that bright floodlight on its pole, she would call loudly for help, scream if necessary. A moment later he would be close to me in the open, away from his phone. That was all I needed.

We reached the point. There he sat as I'd seen him on my two reconnaissances. I saw him lift his tea mug and — without looking at it because his eyes were still sucking in his newspaper's Newsak — take a moderate swallow. She began to rise.

Instantly I realised that it was now she must do it. This was the last moment at which someone would be near her to give her a chance.

The wrench was in my hand — I didn't trust my aim in the dark. Suppose she stumbled screaming away from me. It was less the fear of this that stopped me than a picture of her dented skull, a hollow full of clotted hair and bits of bone and welling blood.

I let it fall with a soft splash into the mud and began to curse softly. We both bent to search, she genuinely passing her open hands about the grass and mud of the ditch bottom, myself pretending to search, my hand busy in my pocket.

It was fifty centimetres long. In each end there were small loops. Through these, ready for tonight, I'd fitted small pieces of wood about half the length of a pencil but twice as thick.

I drew it tight, feeling it settle softly into the flesh of her neck. I heard her sudden cut-off gasp for breath. My right foot slipped in the mud. Both hands busy, I couldn't raise my arms to keep my balance and had only the taut wire to hold on to. The added pressure on it overbalanced both of us. For several seconds we staggered heavily about the muddy ditch before falling together, giving my right knee a violent jolt.

She really struggled then. I should have expected it. As a child I'd shot rabbits and sometimes had to kill a wounded one. Though dying, its hind legs would strike in and out like some huge steel spring and its claws would rip your arm open if you let them. On other occasions a shot one the instant after it was hit would hurl itself a metre and a half into the air. I should have imagined the death contractions of a creature as young and healthy as those rabbits but as large and strong as a human being.

I'm not small or weak myself. For three minutes she threw me about like some tiny attached child. At one point I knelt on her back. She threw me over her head. I held on.

I felt no erotic excitement. Why hide it from myself if I had? I felt horror at what I was doing and anger that she wouldn't die and a desperate desire to get it finished — and anxiety in case I pulled so hard I'd wrench her head off.

She lay still. Panting and gasping, still kneeling, I looked down at her. I could faintly see her open eyes, white in her blacked face. I looked up over the ditch edge. The signalman was taking another moderate sup from his mug. That was how long it had taken: the time between two mouthfuls of tea.

It was downhill, but she was heavy and I often had to move with my knees bent to keep below the tops of the hedges. I held her arms over my shoulders, gripping them above the elbow, but in this position her head was free to loll about on her shoulders and once or twice it rolled forwards and gave the back of my neck a heavy thud. Also my hands were both occupied so I had no way to move branches aside or part fences. Presently I wired her elbows together. Now my hands were free, but I could use them only briefly or the pressure of her tied elbows on my throat stopped my breathing.

Knees shaky with exhaustion, I came to the river bank. In my relief I almost tipped her straight in, but stopped myself in time. I took off her clothes. The hooks and buttons were difficult in the darkness. I began to curse. Was she already stiffening? Taking my knife I began to cut and slice angrily at the cloth. My hands shook so much we were both in danger of getting cut. I made myself stop and count slowly to ten.

When she was naked and I'd recovered her bandolier I dragged her to the bank and slid her in. She floated but nine-tenths submerged. The fast-flowing water dragged at her and a strange pale patch near her head which looked like reeds turned out to be her hair drifting free, but she stuck on shallow mud and I had to wade knee deep and use a stick to poke her free.

I dug quickly with my hands just above the water level and buried her clothes. I had no time to camouflage my work. With luck the water would rise and do it for me.

Undressing myself, I put my own clothes and equipment into the plastic bag I'd brought for such an emergency and before I had a chance to hesitate got into the water.

Naked in this icy torrent, the mouth of my plastic bag

gripped in my teeth, I was quickly carried so far from the shore that it became only an indistinct grey fuzz which I might or might not still be seeing. Almost at once there was no other thought in my mind except, Let me get out of here and be warm and dry and dressed, above all dressed. Till then how can I possibly be heroic?

My pain and shivering rose to a climax beyond which I knew I would cease to fight. I shut my eyes. I tried to hurry this climax forward. An instant later I discovered that I'd somehow survived it and the pain had very slightly eased — though only to begin to build again. Courage and clothes — they are closely connected.

Close to me, Lena's naked body was also being swirled along. Surely a bobbing shape only a couple of metres to my left *was* her? The thought that I might get entangled with her clammy bare limbs nauseated me.

Wisely I'd greased my body with half my weekly edible fat ration — all evening it had been dragging stickily against the insides of my shirt and trousers. I might otherwise not have survived. And luckily my pleading cowardice was useless: swept forward by that bubbling torrent, I didn't even attempt to regain the bank. I could only struggle sideways to try to bring the right-hand pillar of Double Y into my path. I remember no other motive for attempting it than my desire to escape from that icy water at the first possible place.

My numb hands touched slimy stone. This bridge support was vast, I knew — now I could see it reaching high into the night above me — but I'd failed to realise that there was *any* distance between the water level and the top of the pedestal. Was this metre of vertical greasy stone going to defeat me? My hand touched a projection: a line of iron pins. I kept still in the water, not daring to try to climb in case I failed.

I reached the pedestal, dressed and sat shivering where that old construction worker had been photographed with his girl forty years before. I climbed the ladder of metal steps set into the stone which he'd described to me. I reached the track.

Far below me the vast river, lit a faint silver by that layer of cloud which still hid the moon, stretched away in both directions, and though I knew that this enormous mass of water was hurtling towards the sea, once again I had to watch carefully for the occasional churning ripples which broke into foam. Looking along the rails themselves towards the restricted south bank I saw only the blackness of low hills. In the other direction a loom of light showed the position of the signal box, hidden by a slight bend.

Out there at the bridge's centre, high up in the night, it was the quiet that most impressed me. My alertness to any sound seemed to reach out over the surrounding country-side for twenty kilometres in every direction. I felt a curious reluctance to disturb this silent night around me.

Fixing the charges was simple, but there were too few to be trusted. Using the wrench I began to work at the nuts which held one rail end into its metal shoe. I'd not reckoned on the strength it would need or how exhausted I'd be. My knees and arms shook continuously. With ter-rible effort I loosened a bolt, but at once the nut at its other end began to turn too. I needed a second spanner, probably a second person.

As I strained and heaved in the darkness at the next bolt, seeming already to feel the damage it was doing my heart, something made me look up. About ten paces away in the darkness I saw a figure. He was standing completely still and watching me. I had a clear idea of the sudden harsh laugh he was about to give. He might even be taking careful aim, his gun invisibly aligned between us. Would the next thing I felt be a blow which would drive me staggering off the bridge into the black river seventy metres below?

Fifteen seconds passed before this figure made a tiny movement which told me he was facing *away* from me. He moved a few steps then stopped. Far from being watched, *I* was watching him.

Moving and stopping in this uncertain way, giving me more and more the feeling that he'd come on to this bridge to be quiet and alone, he gradually went into the greyness towards the south bank. The whole two or three minutes while he was in sight there was only one desire in my mind: to run and strike this innocent figure from behind with my wrench. Revenge for the shock he'd caused me?

The interruption seemed to take the last of my strength. Fortunately I now saw what I needed: close to the bridge parapet, a low pile of sleepers.

It took me many minutes to get one into position, its end on the rail, the other wedged against a transverse girder. Correct positioning was vital or the wheels of the engine merely brushed it aside . . .

Five hundred metres down stream, where the river brought me to its bank, more driftwood than swimmer, I dressed for the second time. Here I crouched and waited till I dared watch no longer. Dawn was in the sky, but still no train came.

All the way back across the flat lands my ears were alert for that distant rattle which would turn echoey as it reached the bridge and end in two sharp detonations followed by a far away screeching and howling of metal as carriage after carriage went careering through the thin parapet, dragging the next after it. I'd be too far to hear splashes, though perhaps I'd faintly catch the mass screaming of all those trapped soldiers.

I heard nothing.

Nor did I hear radio news of any accident or read of one in the papers on the days which followed. They sometimes report them if they are too big to hide, either as genuine accidents or as acts of sabotage, depending whether the policy is to create calm and confidence or stir up alarm and anger. Perhaps that figure on the bridge returned and found what I'd done. Perhaps I should have trusted my instinct and gone after him. Perhaps Lena — but no, between the time I told her that our operation had been put forward and her death she was never out of my sight.

I've not returned to that bridge. It's a rule they impress on us, knowing how strong this desire will be in the criminal people they've made us.

When friends die, part of ourselves dies. It's a truism. Long ago I passed beyond a competitive but guilty sense of victory that I'd survived them, and felt instead a missing part, an aching loss. Though not perhaps with real pain till my mother died.

For years, of course, she'd been dying on me, a little at a time, whenever I brought her things I'd achieved and noticed how she failed to understand them. I'd turned to others for the praise I badly needed. But often my mind would click back from this more realistic attitude and I'd find it still taking things to her: 'Mother, look, oh look, mother. I'd find it hoping for the warm glow of happiness her praise once gave me — and die a little as I realised that never again could she give it me.

I'd believed I was treating Lena as a child, but I find that little by little I'd begun to bring her things. Never again shall I see her stare of frightened admiring happiness as I tell her about some new plan — for using my carborundum dust, for example — which one day we'll operate together.

Had she been double-crossing me for months? Were they — and she — leaving me free as long as I thought I was undiscovered? If so her disappearance will end my usefulness and my freedom. Every part of me cries out against it. She *did* love me. She *did* hate them. A thousand intimate memories prove it. Our mistake is to expect human beings to be integrated, purposefully directed creatures. I'm not, so why should others be? The consistency and logic we pretend to are all subsequent rationalisation. When the test came Lena didn't suddenly cease to love me or to hate them. She just obeyed some third impulse, some forgotten terror they'd planted in her. This is my belief, and incidentally my only hope.

From which it would follow that I needn't have done it.

I went to work next day, an elementary precaution. Lack of sleep is something I can handle, even the constant anxiety that I'll lose concentration and slip a hand below the oiled silver blade of that two-metre-wide, sixteen-ton guillotine.

All that day Harris seemed to stand behind me, on a raised concrete walk from which he could look directly down on my bench. Whenever I glanced at him I detected a sneer. How had I failed to notice it before? In my mind this sneer grew more and more exaggerated. It drew up the corner of his mouth from inch-long teeth. When I didn't glance back I pictured him no longer on that concrete walk but standing immediately behind me, holding something raised over my head. By four when my shift ended I knew it was no mere lack of sleep I was suffering from. I had a high fever.

I set out for home. I went in the most astonishing way, swaying and zigzagging, bumping along the fronts of houses at one moment, half off the pavement into the street at the next. There seemed nothing I could do to stop it. At any second I'd be picked up as a drunk. I was less walking than going in a crumpled stumble, my bent and shaky knees continuously on the verge of collapsing completely beneath me.

My new hotel was only three short streets from the factory gate. I remember that journey going on for street after street, hour after hour. Often I was on the sunny side but knew I hadn't the smallest chance of crossing. The dizzying sun brought sweat running out of my hair, down my face and neck. My shirt was sodden. My trousers felt so clammy I was surprised not to see wet black patches on them. Bed, bed, my mind cried. Just as, in the river it had been reduced to a single desire for clothes, so now it contained nothing but a longing to close my eyes and lie for ever on something soft. Soon I'd use the pavement. Even that idea ceased to alarm me.

All night I sweated. My sweat seemed to make pools in which I lay but at the same time I shivered so heavily that my teeth knocked together. There were pains in my chest. No doubt I had pneumonia. I took substitute aspirin, all you can buy off prescription. I lost count of the number I'd taken.

Suppose I couldn't go to work. A doctor's visit, the loss of my job, investigation.

I had a high . . . Must be a hundred, hundred . . . No way . . . Alone . . .

My light was on but several hours had surely passed. I believed I'd left the thoughts I'd been having lying around, exposed for any visitor to discover them. I was out of bed, swaying about. I knelt to stop myself falling, but still struggled to remember what I had to hide. My mind clicked straight. With a small laugh I got back into bed and turned off the light.

People came into the room. They spoke to each other about me but I couldn't answer or move. They were detached, judging, not unkind.

Jane. And a doctor. A child too, a little boy of perhaps four. He was familiar. He was the child I'd hoped Jane and I would one day have. He was also the child I myself had once been. I call these dreams but because I was awake they had a different quality from any others I remember. For one thing, though I tried to make them go away I couldn't.

Morning came. I was no better, but I didn't dare stay at home when their enquiries about Lena would be at their height. I sat on the floor, my trousers half on, my head resting on my knees, moaning aloud that I couldn't go on because of the appalling headache dressing had given me. An instant later I was propping myself against my work bench. Memo to Judd, that overgrown boy scout: among these amphetamines, gripe, anti-gripe, sleeping and suicide tablets, why not a basic anti-biotic course?

Next day I was better. The pain in my chest had eased — I'd coughed up several frothy green gouts of phlegm. The day after I was dizzy and weak again.

I was in the canteen. I stood in the queue, not daring to raise my eyes to the girls in white caps behind the service counter. I moved away carrying tea mug and bun plate, eyes down, jostled by lurching figures in blue denim overalls. Starting with my eyes down it seemed impossible to look up or I'd find every one of these pushing people staring at the curious sleepwalking creature I must appear. At last I found an empty table in a far corner, sat,

94

and did raise my eyes . . . Someone was coming to join me. 'Sorry,' I began, as if to pretend the other chair was taken. 'Morning, Meyer.' It was Harris.

He didn't wear overalls, but a big shabby dark suit, very out of shape as if for years heavy things had hung in its pockets, though not actually frayed or stained. My fishmonger, I remembered, had worn a striped apron. He'd used it for wiping his red scaley hands. Harris also has big red hands. Flopped there on the green formica beside the ketchup bottle, they were the hands of a promoted artisan which however much he scrubs them will never go back to shape. He seemed entirely unconscious of my failure to answer him.

'Service,' he called suddenly and loudly — not in the way a worker would, except perhaps as a jokey flirtation, more as if the sight of the stinking unemptied ashtray on our table made him remember his executive status. Looking directly into my eyes without any expression he said more quietly, 'Wouldn't have happened in Lena's time.'

So you'd rather have her mentioned, he seemed to be saying, straightfaced but laughing. It was true, I'd been longing for someone to speak about her. Their silence had become unbearable. Where's old Lena? I wanted them to say. It was as if only when they'd said it and then forgotten her could I forget her. But not Harris.

'That's right,' I began, and choked. A phlegmy blockage in my throat had made it start an octave too high. Clutching my chest as if I needed the toilet to spit into, I left him.

Was he homosexual? Was he trying to set up a relationship with me? Did my trapped condition excite him? That and many other possibilities were in my mind as I hurried through the subterranean passage back to work. Near its lowest point I tripped and only saved myself from falling flat by clutching at the side wall.

As I stood there recovering my breath, my mind still so filled by frightening speculation that I half expected at any second to feel his hand on my shoulder, hardly seeing all those overalled workers surging past, I realised that someone else *was* near me. Just at my back, leaning against the same wall.

'You all right?'

'Yes yes,' I said, pushed myself free, and stood swaying indiotically.

'This way.'

She took me to the first-aid desk. I'd scraped the skin off my knuckles. There wasn't much damage but a lot of blood.

All that day I kept thinking of her unasked kindness. And of what she'd said at my bench before she'd left me there, glancing anxiously back as if wondering whether she should. 'Right of the main gate. Four-fifteen.'

She brought me home. She stayed the night.

Short, thickly built, with freckles which spread down her neck on to her shoulders but fade above her breasts and long black hair that falls down her bare back almost to her buttocks and little stubby fingers — I'd already made love to Annya before I noticed her fingers, no doubt because she often keeps her small fists closed. They have no nails.

Now I hear her feet in the corridor outside my room, quick, busy, no one would guess . . . A month has passed since Annya spent that first night with me. Tonight I've decided that I shall trust her.

2

SCARS too, but because they're mostly dotted white lines, suggesting bicycle chains, neither did I notice these at first. They're on her back and buttocks and belly and thighs, as if she's been hung up by her wrists and hit from all sides.

She belonged to the Youth League, but when I try to discover exactly who they are she becomes abstracted. 'They're kinky.' It's as if she doesn't want to think about them in case it starts old feelings she can't control. For my sake.

One night she had a revelation — her word — about the sort of people they were and her life with them. Seven or eight of them were jumping in turn with their heavy ornate boots on the hands of a sixty-five-year-old grey-haired curfew-breaker — she ran to the police. She hadn't made the connection I've made, that the police and the Youth League are on the same side.

They pretended to believe her. They made arrests, brought nominal prosecutions, assured her they'd give her protection. Unfortunately the Leaguers got her.

They broke her — her word again. She withdrew her story. She discovered her basic cowardliness. The razor, her face: Like us to draw pictures on you, dearie? Worse, she discovered that she enjoyed her degraded condition.

She talks about this more openly — they could hardly object. She's an advertisement for their methods. If she ever became dangerous again they'd crack the whip and she'd come running.

She describes the 'White' — Youth Leader — in rings and silver-studded jacket, who did it. She doesn't pretend to love him in the normal sense. In a flat voice she gives descriptions of him which make him hateful. She's just related to him. It was he who gave her an awakening about herself she couldn't have had any other way.

She tried to faint but she couldn't. She would willingly have confessed anything, given away every friend, abandoned every belief, but she'd done all that. It was when she realised that there wasn't another thing he wanted her to say but he was still beating her that she began to love him. Not in an abstract way. Sexually. She saw him no longer as repulsive but beautiful. At the same time that she was suffering worse pain than she'd thought possible she was the victim of wave after wave of longing for him. Why, oh why wouldn't he love her? Her belly, her whole self kept uncontrollably opening itself for him. Now she hated him for *not* taking her, but at the same time enjoyed being digusting to him.

For perhaps a year she stayed around them, indulging in the punishment of being treated as scum. It's only in the last six months that she's tried to escape by taking a secretarial job at this factory. She doesn't believe it can last. 'If they whistle,' she says.

And her fingernails? Too systematic, I guess. More likely she was born without them, or as a child chewed them down to these almost non-existent little rims of cartilage. Her nails are probably a cause, not a result, of her time with the Youth League. If they hadn't made her unlovable she'd never have flung herself at them in the way I suspect she did.

She gives me a feeling no one else ever has, that the idea we carry with us from birth and preserve long after experience and reason should have taught us better, that life has nice treats in store for us, she has truly abandoned. She expects only more of what it has already given her: unhappiness, relieved by ironic moments of eroticism.

She's discovered conclusively that she can't be the person she would like to be — the two are irreconcilable. With a ruthless but intuitive logic she's realised that this leaves her no basis for anything except stoicism.

Annya making love: I've never known anything like it. She howls, sobs, clutches me, tears at my back with her nail-less fingers, cries at me to hurt her more, more. She moans, gasps, shudders. She throws back her head so her short freckled throat is taut. Oh Alec, oh Alec, oh God, oh Christ, oh Jesus. Her legs thrash about. Her whole body humps and writhes and tosses. Once she threw me right out of her and — because I was off balance — half to the floor. I was on the point of laughing, when I saw her face. It was rigid, postponing every emotion till this accident was put right. That too was comic, but I didn't laugh.

When it's finished she holds me in her arms and croons at me as if I were a baby: 'Poor Alec, poor Alec — meaning poor Annya?

I remember these things in a cool detached way, but at the time I'm not detached. This strange animal who has no connection with the talking, reasoning Annya I know, is wonderful. I also moan and cry. The only thing I prevent myself doing is laughing aloud with happiness because that too might be misunderstood.

My error with Lena lay in persuading myself that she would never betray me. I don't make the same mistake with Annya. From the first, long before I recruited her, she was warning me.

'I can tell you because I'm harmless,' she says — about

her Youth League experience. 'If they threatened me I'd deny every word.'

The strange thing is that, beyond the person she believes she has become I sense a person who has *not* been destroyed, who stands apart from her own superficial judgment of herself, who will one day recreate her independence, unless of course they kill her first.

'Do you feel no resentment?'

She talks about the rightness of submitting to a life-force greater than her own. These aren't her words. They're party words. They've reduced her to a talking shell with a tape of clichés. If I can make her play this tape often enough it may bring nearer the surface what's below.

As a secretary Annya works inside that so-called administrative block. She's ideally placed to help me. Till I met her my progress with my main mission seemed blocked. She is also helping me about Harris. Alone one's judgment can go wrong. I need a second opinion.

Once or twice a week now, whether I sit at a canteen table or stand against the wall, he brings his morning coffee to drink with me. Three days ago he suggested we meet one day after work. Looking straight at me, he gave me this invitation in exactly the words he once used to Lena. 'Like a night out?' It was so familiar I almost added, 'ducks', to remind him.

Long before I'd finished telling Annya she began to shake her head as if she didn't want to know. I had to make her listen.

She stood facing my bed, forcing me to go to its far side and talk to her across it. She went and stood facing a wall — I pushed myself between her and the wall. She still looked down at the floor. I took her naked freckled shoulders in my hands, compelling her to look up at me and understand.

'What's the use?' I heard her mutter. She was like someone who has been drowned and sees her body lying on the beach with people working on it, and suffers — so it's said — appalling agony as she's drawn back into it.

'That's not the point,' I told her. 'You can't ask that.'

'Oh no!' she said, still quietly but bitterly.

I made her understand. She began to nod fast and at the same time, grabbing my wrist, to pull me towards the bed. She pulled hard, almost frantically. Usually we wait longer.

3

WE must enter the administrative block. Annya agrees.

Not in day-time when it's open for inspection, camouflage in place, but at night; not the public part where she works but the secret area which surely exists beyond. And which part of this should we check first? The office of our labour relations officer, I suggested, and explained his codename to her. She shrugged then nodded. Two days ago — a disturbing coincidence — our plans were disrupted. I was put on night shift.

Now I work during those evening hours we'd hoped to use. Although Annya could linger behind after her day's work and let me in soon afterwards, she could hardly hang about the women's lavatory for eight hours till my shift ends at midnight.

It has also disrupted my night information-gathering which, since I met Annya, I had begun again. On these nights I'd sleep from four-thirty in the afternoon till eleven then rise fresh and rested for my real work. Now, arriving home at twelve-fifteen, I am in no condition for several hours of concentrated scouting, when one slip could prove fatal. But as if to prove something to myself I determined last night to go. I would take Annya.

She was waiting in my room, playing with a little skinny kitten she has found in the hotel corridor. I suspected that for all the seven hours she'd been waiting for me, she'd been playing with him.

I told her my plan.

'He's called Mr. Pete,' she said.

I told her I needed her help — not true, but I did want to test her in action.

'Mr. Pete's hungry,' she said. 'Nasty men don't look after him.'

Astonishingly, quite silencing me, she began to cry. Not openly — she kept her face down to the cat — but unmistakably. I suspected it was surprising her too.

She held his tail provocatively. Instantly he whisked through a hundred and eight degrees and set his teeth in the back of her hand. I guessed how painful this must be, but her face showed no pain, though now that she'd raised it I saw the tears on it more clearly. Beside her knee I saw dry crusts of bread — she'd brought him some of her ration.

I offered her a sweater, saying it got chilly at dawn. I was about to mention burnt cork for face blacking. Crouching there on the floor, still not looking at me, her rather plump buttocks and thighs naked on the worn carpet — she was wearing only a short black blouse — she suddenly began to shake her whole head and neck in a strange shivering way. At the same second — perhaps she heard it first — from below my window came the most hideous Youth League screeching I'd yet heard, followed by a stampede of steel-studded boots, then a great shout of pain and the words, 'No, no, no, no,' getting fainter. My hand went to my gun. At least I could kill a few. Perhaps I'd have gone if it hadn't occurred to me that the whole thing might not be an outrage but a mock-up of an outrage, a merry titillating imitation of the real victim they'd failed to find.

I went without Annya. Now the moonlit streets were silent and deserted, but all the time I crept along the house fronts of the outskirts of the town I still thought about the Youth League and the way the Visitors are handing over more and more of their terrorising, especially the keeping of the curfew, to such brutal teenage gangs. The apparent freedom these creatures enjoy keeps them behaving in the desired pattern — they even believe they're attacking the system. In fact they're one of its main supports, reinforcing the collaborators in their loyalty, who see police and Visitors alike as their only protection. From Nazi times children have been used systematically against parents. This is an ingenious refinement.

As always, music is the most important device for stirring and captivating such immature youth and here technology has made the process simpler. Parades, rallies and marches with brass bands and uniforms are no longer needed. Instead all day, swaggering brainlessly up and down the streets, they carry their own radios which pour the required jungle music into their heads. Their over-developed muscles are controlled by brains reduced to sounding boxes for native rhythms.

Out on the flat lands, spreading away from me for many kilometres in the moonlight, I saw again the ruined shapes of many of the farms and their outbuildings. At night their superficial patching and the removal of rubble no longer deceived me. Dark and lifeless — by now it was one in the morning — they looked abandoned.

Something had also changed about the countryside itself. On my early summer reconnaissances I'd been alert for signs of the Maquis and often had a strong sense that they were all around me, the woods full of them, watching for the moment when they felt sure enough of my identity to reveal themselves. Now I sensed that these resistance fighters had moved away to another part of the country — no, that's too specific, more that they'd faded or grown still. As if what I'd once detected had turned out to be merely grass rustling in the wind.

Perhaps it was the bleakness of the scene across which I seemed to move with difficulty like some injured insect which set me thinking how little I'd so far achieved except to survive. Even here I had barely exceeded the average. In a Restricted File at Ops I'd once discovered a statistical analysis — not the sort of thing they showed us — which gave seven months as the average survival time in our area. At first it had been much less, but that was before we were properly trained. What worried the writer of this analysis was that although there had once been a steady improvement, this had levelled off and now neither better training nor better equipment seemed to produce longer average survival. It was as if there was some allotted span beyond which the odds on discovery became overwhelming, or agents just grew tired and made mistakes — he expressed it in more professional jargon.

I found myself remembering my earliest meeting with Colonel Judd. I remembered his big grey head and the sense that he was flattering me by interviewing me at all so I'd better quickly prove I deserved it or he'd switch off, not become hostile, just impatient for someone more hopeful. I believe he took me because he detected that I was terrified by the waste of my life, though it's hard to imagine him putting such a thing into words without so embarrassing himself he'd have become a sort of vibrating steam pudding. My safe job in which from nine-thirty to six each day I spoke the language of war but was never touched by it, my gay love for Jane so totally and sadly its own end — he was right, but it was something I'd meant to hide from him.

Around four a.m. as I slogged forwards across ankle-twisting ploughed stubble, near exhaustion from my day's work and night's patrol, I thought so much of Judd that he seemed to speak to me. Not literally, of course, but I experienced a strange direct contact with him, and an intimation of all that he'd once hoped for me. It was as if he'd been trying to pass this information all night, but was only now coming through loud and clear. I was ashamed of my despair.

I looked on the bright side — itself a stammering Judd cliché: my new shift had allowed me to postpone my night on the town with Harris. I remembered half a dozen things I'd so far not tried: my carborundum dust.

Dawn was in the sky when I left the arterial road and turned for home. All the way back it grew brighter. As I came into the alley behind the hotel I had a strange sense of something happening above me and, looking up, saw the telegraph wires thick with swallows.

Thousands of them. Amazing to think that this vast hoard had been spread over the countryside all summer. My presence set a group of them into flight and this in turn startled another. Soon the whole sky was full of wheeling, screaming, rising, realighting parties. I hurried indoors. I hadn't realised that summer was so far gone.

Annya was asleep on my bed. I had to wake her and

make her leave quickly. The kitten had gone, though it had left behind a smell. I like the pleasure he gives her though I suspect he's a risk.

'Sales Department!' I said to her as she left, thinking of the part of the organisation she works in. 'Why do they need a Sales Department?'

'Sales and *Distribution*,' she said. 'That's what it mostly does.' But she agreed that the word Sales was astonishing, accidentally surviving perhaps from before the war, when it was a commercial light engineering factory. Or intentionally retained as a cover to suggest it wasn't doing war work. Thin, I said, unless to bluff whoever guessed it into searching no deeper.

Stopping in the doorway, she looked back at me with surprise, as if she'd thought she knew me but I'd showed an insight she hadn't expected.

I clocked in at four, and at once reported sick. It was alarmingly direct but it might work. As soon as I came back through the main entrance into the yard I turned sharply left and ducked behind the group of concrete waste-product vats which stand here waiting to be hauled away.

Crouching among these four-foot white cylinders I expected at any second to hear the howling siren of a squad car or some loud shout from close above me, 'Come out there, you.' Nothing happened. Even when I presently peered round my vat I half fancied I might see waiting police, guns raised. The yard was empty and quiet.

Most of the loading is done by night, but at the far side a single lorry was parked in one of the despatch bays and two men were lazily filling it with a consignment of crates. The casual way they did this sickened me. They slouched, laughed, bumped the crates, even disappeared for ten minutes behind the warehouse sliding door where they thought they couldn't be seen but where faint drifts of cigarette smoke gave them away. I'd have been less angry if they'd been brisk and dedicated. I wanted to yell at them that those bombs and shell casings they were so thoughtlessly loading would soon be killing and wounding the soldiers who were fighting to free them.

It's the same at work, there are days when I can hardly bear to keep silent. Don't you understand what you're doing? I want to shout at them as they stand, eyes down at their machines, working with steady care. The hard workers seem not even to suffer the normal guilt such workers feel that they are being disloyal to their mates. Nor do the lazy ones draw attention to their clever sloth, as they would surely once have done, confident that it would be seen as class solidarity. Is it possible that this acquiescence which they've reverted to, now that trade unions have been transformed into state unions, is a more natural human condition?

The signal came at last: a vertical line of toilet paper suspended inside the semi-opaque glass of the women's lavatories of the administrative block. Annya had reached her first objective. I came quickly into the open — there was no other way to cross the yard — and walked confidently towards the ramp which led down to the doors of the boiler house.

All those fifty metres the flesh between my shoulder blades where our ancestors used to expect knife or spear blades squirmed. There were seconds when I had the dreamlike sensation that I was walking and walking but getting no nearer. Reaching the ramp the desire to run those last few paces became almost uncontrollable. I controlled it and descended at the same steady rate. The door opened to my pull and I stepped quickly into total blackness smelling thickly of fuel oil.

At once I moved sideways from the position in which I would last have been visible as a silhouette in the doorway, at which a gun might still be being aimed. I bumped a heavy obstacle . . . Annya.

Gripping my hand, she began to pull me deeper into the blackness, her eyes it seemed already adapted, under pipes coated in scorching asbestos which cascaded dust on to us as we brushed below them. We'd only gone five or six paces when some huge furnace began a fierce whirring hiss. A second later it fired and a shuddering roar filled the whole of this low space. Through it we now hurried so clumsily that I tripped on a crate, fell to my knees and lost my hold. Groping for her, my hand touched something soft and warm, drew away . . . her knee. Quickly she pulled me into a low recess.

This space was so small that our shoulders and hips were pressed together. For an hour we crouched there, waiting till the last of the administrative staff would have left. Sometimes the furnaces were silent and we could whisper, sometimes they roared and shuddered so we could only communicate by touch. In those long moments I became aware, even through the smell of furnace oil, of Annya's breath. It had the same bitter smell that Lena's used to have.

Softly we came up concrete steps to the ground floor. Here we reached marble corridors of great height, late gestures of an age which still believed their machines honoured principles, before ants'-nest utility became general. At the end of one there was a ten-metre-tall orange and brown stained-glass window, the evening sun glowing through its spanners and brawny forearms. Inside these tall chambers of space there was complete silence except when our feet made tiny scrapes or clicks and set up hugely magnified echoes. If someone at the farthest side of this mausoleum-like labyrinth had cleared his throat I believe we should have heard it clearly. To everything I was acutely alert. At last after so many months I was penetrating the primary objective of my mission. And it was easy.

I was full of conceit at the way I'd waited so patiently for the right contact. How clever, meanwhile, to have found a room which gave me a direct view of the building's car park and main entrance, where in the past weeks I'd seen enough comings and goings of administrators to convince me that this was no normal office complex. These last days in particular, when for the first time I'd been at home in the mornings and early afternoons, I'd watched the arrival of carload after glossy carload.

The instant they stopped all four doors would spring wide as if some internal catch had been tripped and those heavy dark-suited men would stride in pairs away up concrete paths with controlled urgent purpose, their shoulders a little hunched, their hands gripped behind their backs — no general ever put his hands in his pockets. At heart he's still the cadet who would have got screamed at if he had. What small things betray people.

Watching them — indirectly, using my bedroom mirror like an Amsterdam whore — I was at last sure what I was looking at: a hidden army headquaters. Perhaps *the* Visitors' headquarters. The exact nature of my mission — always left flexible to depend on what I discovered — grew clearer. In the so-called boardroom of this block, at the time of the Rev or Second Coming, a well-aimed grenade or burst of sten-gun fire might do more to dislocate their organisation than a dozen thousand-bomber raids. Simple — perhaps too simple.

If this was all, couldn't I have been told? Dimly I suspected that there was something less obvious housed in this block, something I would sabotage merely by discovering its true nature. I shied away from calling it a secret weapon, so suggesting some new laser beam, gas culture or automated battlefield technology. I pictured something more evil. Some brain or principle. It was vague but getting clearer.

Annya led me by a service lift to the second floor — she'd prepared well. We still saw no one. Now, at the hour of the evening meal had been the right time to come. She led me down less pretentious corridors of offices formed by glass partitions. In my pocket I checked my wires and talc plates — a part of our training I'd taken seriously. Again she gripped my wrist to lead me softly and cautiously forwards. She pointed to the door itself.

My wires were actually touching the lock when, glancing up, I saw clearly through the frosted glass panel of the door the shape of a man sitting at the desk inside.

In turn we peered through the keyhole. Harris. He wasn't reading or writing but sitting upright, hands side by side on the desk edge, looking down at something on its surface: cards. He was playing patience.

We moved softly away. We checked corridors on other floors and tested closed doors, but I didn't try to unlock them. The discovery of him sitting there had confused us. I blame myself for having prepared no alternative. I'm surprised that I didn't improvise one. Somehow the problem of what it meant absorbed my thoughts.

Almost my only recollection of those upper corridors, which had at first seemed as silent as the ones below, is that they were being shaken by a heavy continuous vibration. Was the steady grinding of the factory, by then halfway through the first night shift, more audible up there? Certainly, as we descended to the boiler room I ceased to hear it.

We have returned to my room. Annya is feeding bread crusts to Mr. Pete. He gets one into the back corner of his mouth and champs at it, showing his long teeth, transforming his sweet pussy face into something unpleasantly carnivorous. We don't talk much. It's as if we have neither of us yet found self-protecting words to describe tonight's fiasco. Though I watch Annya squatting there, again undressed below the waist, she doesn't look at me but looks down at Mr. Pete. She teases him till he drops his crust and snarls at her. She gives it back to him and strokes him. If she did look up my instinct would be to look away.

She takes off her black blouse. She's short, heavy — and beautiful. It's what I've thought for a long time. Now it needs an effort for me to realise that to others her broad freckled face is plain, because to me it's just as beautiful as her big breasts and big thighs and wide hips with their fine curves ... A conventionally pretty face on top of these would be as grotesque as something in a game of consequences.

4

By next day I knew I'd exaggerated the implications of the incident. A good labour relations officer might be around the factory at any hour of the day or night, impressing his workers by his dedication. Nonetheless, I felt an illogical anxiety about the moment when I would next meet him, increased by his absence the following evening; and yesterday when at last I knew he had emerged on the concrete walk behind my bench I broke into a heavy sweat.

'One of us.' All last night I tried to apply my intuition to discovering. I looked for a certain carelessness in his attitude towards himself and an exceptional care of other people. I looked for my own split vision: a full enjoyment of life which at the same time I see as infinitesimally short and totally futile. An indulgent laughter at myself which is part of my enjoyment and doesn't take away from it. Both alternatives I would find unbearable, total involvement or permanent immobilising laughter.

So my question expanded confusingly beyond an attempt to guess whether he was an agent, trained and employed by our organisation, and became the question Jane and I would ask about a new casual seaside acquaintance. Did he have our values? I was never ashamed of the implication that we believed we were superior. So we did and should.

Last night about Harris I seemed continuously on the point of answering, Yes. I imagined the mask dissolving. In his eyes I saw warm approval of the way I'd survived these months of isolation. A second later I was deeply suspicious of something I so much hoped for.

Had Lena been one of us? Perhaps I never asked because I don't believe women are capable of my double vision. They would consider it cynical, shifting their minds with difficulty to such a concept, committing themselves to nothing because they secretly believed I could only be inventing such an absurdity to flirt with them.

All night Harris's labrador face, capped by his ill-concealed bald patch, changed shape and meaning for me . . .

It became a worrying part of that distorted scene which the night shift often presents. By day I'd found nothing unusual in these bent overalled men isolated at their machines in this deafening roar. At night looking round this same roaring yellow cavern, aware of the silent streets and sleeping town outside, I suddenly feel I'm being shown some grotesque fantasy. 'Not just a stranger world than we think, but stranger than we *can* think,' as some modern Rutherford has said. He seemed to accept it without resentment. I can't. To have been granted only sufficient intelligence to guess that our intelligence is insufficient. Last night, more than ever before I was convinced that I was this sort of groping creature, able to make a little sense of local phenomena, knowing that the overall enemy scheme was beyond my comprehension.

Towards ten I became practical. I watched the doorway to the room used by the maintenance engineers.

It's a small room, constructed of oily grey planks which separate it from the rest of the machine-shop floor. During the day there's either some white-overalled mechanic leaning in it's doorway or I can see the feet of others who are drinking tea inside. They have privileges. Now both doorway and room beyond seemed empty. I guessed that at night it was only manned by a skeleton staff.

Through the doorway, suspended along the front edge of a shelf of oil cans, I could see ten or a dozen grease guns.

The moment the bell sounded for our second break I moved quickly along an aisle of capstans so that my route to the canteen took me close to the maintenance room door. Instead of passing I stepped inside.

If I'd found someone in there I'd have asked him to look at my trimmer which had developed a vibration. I found no one. Quickly I slid the nearest grease gun through my flies into my trouser leg, gripped it with a hand in my pocket, rezipped and emerged again. I'd been so quick that I was able to join the slower workers still filing towards the canteen.

But at the entrance to the subterranean tunnel I turned into the gents and locked myself in a toilet. I couldn't keep one hand in my pocket for the remaining two hours of my shift. Quickly I used my prepared strips of handkerchief to bind the gun to my leg below the knee.

I was lucky. As soon as I reached home I unscrewed its cap and found it three-quarters full of grease. Using my knife I extracted half a kilo of this and mixed into it a small heap of carborundum dust.

It was like a delicate piece of cookery. First I cut it in, then, using the flat of the blade, gently pressed the soft mass into a mound, and only finally stirred with the point. I returned the grease in knifeloads, wiped the plate with my finger till not the tiniest black smear remained and cleaned my finger on the inside rim of the gun's barrel. The mixing of that grey powder into the soft brown grease gave me a strange excitement. Such a tiny action, such a vast power for destruction.

By the time I hid the gun in my bottom drawer it was almost full daylight. I'd used only a quarter of my dust. This evening when I return this gun I may borrow another.

My only company has been the sleeping Mr. Pete — that's his habit when Annya isn't here. Despite her care he's still a small skinny ball with fur which never lies smooth but stands out scruffily. Sometimes he changes position, eyes me with what I consider excessive disappointment and curls himself into a new ball.

Tomorrow night Annya will be here, but I shall say

nothing till I have real news for her. Lately there's been too much talk and too little successful action.

Far quicker and more dramatic than I'd imagined. To-night, only three nights since I rehung it on its shelf below the oil cans, the moment I came on to the machine-shop floor I saw that one of the big capstans near the fire exit was deserted. Within an hour two others had stopped. I actually heard the bearings of one go with a big jud-dering screech followed by a low sputtering and a little column of blue smoke.

The hours which followed were the best since my drop. Suddenly I was no longer botching my part. I knew just how long to work on as if I'd noticed nothing and just the glassy-eyed surprise to show when a group of half a dozen mechanics was joined by three dark-suited ill-tempered executives. Presently, as if it wasn't my affair, I began to feed my big guillotine again, but I was filled with the happiness of a job well done. Last night I was unbeatable.

I told Annya. It was worth waiting for. She looked up from the floor and stared. Again she was realising how she'd underestimated me.

'They're so inefficient,' I said. 'A child could have done it.'

'Don't you believe it,' she said.

Odd how it seemed to make her hate them more, hate them *because* they'd failed. She asked me to describe it in detail, as if she wanted to go on thinking about it. Those angry executives, dragged from their black-market cham-pagne suppers. Those bemused mechanics, shitting their pants in alarm — her description — none daring to be the first to make excuses in case it drew attention to him. Several times she interrupted me with harsh humourless laughs. The picture in her mind seemed even more dramatic than the reality.

'It's a start.' I wanted to redirect her gently towards our real objective.

She crossed to the window and pushed aside the heavy blackout curtains. Instinctively I clicked off the light switch. Presently I could see her dark shape against the grey V of night sky she'd exposed. She was looking directly towards our factory.

'What does go on in there?'

She didn't answer. Perhaps we'd asked ourselves too often. Perhaps she was sorry I'd broken the flow of her anger.

'Got a new job,' she said.

'You ...?' Had she needed darkness before she could tell me? Had this been the real cause of her anger?

'Harris.' Now she turned into the room.

'You mean ...?'

'I'm his secretary.'

How did it happen? I asked her. She'd received an office letter in an office envelope. Did he personally select her? Impossible to tell. Today, her first, he'd treated her with distant watchfulness, as if not wanting to welcome her as his new girl till he was sure she was.

It was better than anything we could have hoped, I said. It was the breakthrough we had been needing. That was right, she said. Were we reassuring each other?

Isn't it *too* lucky? It's as if someone is holding out luck to us for the fun of seeing us leap around with happiness before he puts a foot on us.

5

'I HATE him,' Annya says. 'He's loathsome. He's slimy.' I thought of those two together?

A week has passed. A most disturbing week.

I suffer acute jealousy — it's the word that comes automatically — of the eight hours a day they spend together, locked in a private hate from which I'm excluded. How close my feelings are to those I used to have about Jane and Hubby. I knew he disgusted her. I still writhed at the thought of them together all evening, all night. In that association there had to be some understanding, for Jane indeed an agreement to submit to his slobbery kisses and clammy handling if he wasn't to become suspicious.

In the same way Annya must simulate loyalty, even enthusiasm for Harris's work on political screening. That's what it is, she's discovered. All that floor-walking, all those invitations to bring him complaints about the canteen coffee, are a cover. His real job is to keep files on every employee and check them for loyalty.

I have asked Annya to look at mine but they're stored in a central system and Harris only gets out those he currently needs. I've suggested she orders mine by its number, and after looking at it returns it saying it was an error, but the fact that she *could* do this, that he *doesn't* keep his employee code numbers secret, suggests that he may have alerted the filing clerks to report exactly this sort of minor irregularity.

Today, sitting in my airless room, I had a sense of growing danger. These mornings when I no longer work and cannot sleep have become increasingly difficult. Every time I glanced at my mirror some new party seemed to be arriving or leaving the main doors of the administrative block. Surely there was a new urgency about their manner.

I found myself saying half aloud to myself, Time is short, time is short; and on another occasion, Short, shorter, shortest . . .

By midday I couldn't spend another minute sitting importently there. I remembered a training suggestion from Major Biggs, voice of Judd, made with a sneering irony as if the mere mention of religion caused him a psychic convulsion. If we were ever desperate we might as a last resort contact the local priest.

I knew the nearest church — St. Clotilde's. I found its rectory a few doors away behind a small front garden of evergreen shrubs in grey sand. A female housekeeper of at least seventy with a club foot led me into a study of many books, thick with pipe smoke. The priest sat at a desk beyond this pale stirring smokescreen through which his round face showed clearly but only a dim outline of his robed shoulders. He grinned.

The relief of that grin. I longed to begin at once to make the comments which all the time rage inside me on his spiritless defeated fellow countrymen. In his presence I could even have risen above my anger and pitied them, accepting the fact that, but for a few awkward genes and the luck of being born in a free country, I might be no better.

But I could say none of these things because of his housekeeper. Instead of shutting the door and leaving us alone she stayed in the passage in full view. More disturbing, whenever I glanced back she was making astonishing signals to the priest, screwing up her eyes, gesturing at my back, mouthing words.

I tried to ignore her and make general conversation. I spoke about the weather — safe — the high cost of food — less safe — the war — risky. He answered politely but with growing surprise at this undirected sequence which became broken by longer and longer gaps as I began to grasp rather desperately at ideas for extending it. Finally a pause arrived which went on and on. Not a single idea remained in my head. Frail ones which I might have used casually if I'd thought of them earlier would after all this silence have had preposterous emphasis.

'So what can I do for you?'

On the point of inventing a problem of conscience or contraception to put to him, I suddenly suspected his tone of phoney priestly optimism. At the same instant I recognised those words as the start of a general emergency password sequence of five answering remarks. With a knocking heart I gave the second of these.

'Oh, there's plenty of time.'

Less than you think, he should have replied, but he didn't. Instead he seemed to understand it literally and, as a result, no longer to hide his irritation at the way I apparently intended to extend my visit into his lunch hour. His manner became cool, even sharp. He glanced at his watch. He glanced at his desk to suggest that down there in the smoke he had work to do.

'I see you're busy,' I said and hurried out ignoring his protests, barging past his housekeeper who was making a signal which consisted of covering her whole face with her hands but peering through slits between her ancient bony fingers. I was two streets away before I guessed that she might be an alcoholic, hanging about in that passage because my visit was preventing her claiming her ration from the priest's sideboard.

As I hurried home through the humid afternoon below

the heavy black clouds of a gathering autumn thunderstorm, I saw my mission in perspective. When I came it had been spring. Even after the disaster of our drop the difficulties of my job had seemed exaggerated, especially when I found Lena. At the worst I had my capsule. Death was terrifying and inevitable, but remote.

This early confidence had lasted me through the long hot summer. I lost Lena. Blackness of spirit followed. But I found Annya and felt a new assurance that I could survive disaster. Perhaps life is like this: the longer we live the nearer death comes, but the habit of living makes it increasingly incredible.

Now it was autumn. In a few weeks it would be winter. Autumn is short, they say, in this country.

Mr. Pete had died. He was on the pavement below my window. I didn't go close but I knew it was him. I pictured him turning over and over in the air, his little fragile legs held still, not trying to fight it. No doubt he'd been exploring my window ledge, looking for Annya.

A few people were gathered round him, but when I looked down from my window a minute later they'd gone. I thought that he had gone too, then saw a small grey mark in the gutter where one of them must have moved him with a shoe.

That night as soon as I came off shift I dropped my aerial out of my window — I'd rescued ten metres on the night of my escape from the Patrases by a sharp jerk which broke it near the chimney stack — and began to transmit. It was so long since I'd done it that my morse was awkward and too full of unintentional errors for me to bother with the checks and bluff checks. I could only hope that something genuine in the flavour of my message would convince them. 'AJAX CALLING AJAX CALLING CONTACT URGENTLY CONFIRM FIELD

BRIEFING ITEM ONE DISCOVERIES IMMI-
NENT WHAT ACTION QUERY.' I went on repeating
these last words over and over. Tapping them steadily into
the night somehow gave me confidence that there were
still people on our side listening, even if something prevented them answering. But, as if the idea provoked its
opposite, I also thought how my evidence that they still
exist has grown increasingly remote. Every public com-
muniqué and news story could be an inspired invention,
part of the oldest totalitarian technique of creating unity
by fostering a sense of danger. Suddenly there was a power
cut.

Now that the days are growing shorter we're getting
these. Coal stocks must be saved for winter, we're told.
They're needed for the munitions industry and mustn't be
squandered by the public. It could be true. Drawing back
my curtain I saw that although the administrative block
was a great hulk of blacker darkness, a loom of light still
showed round the factory itself. But there were also sub-
dued lights in other non-industrial parts of the town. It
confirmed my fear: since I'd last transmitted their detec-
tion techniques had so improved that in a few seconds
they could locate the town of origin of a message. By
cutting the power in that town a section at a time and
seeing which cut stopped a transmission they could
narrow their search to a few streets.

As I stood there in the darkness there were unfamiliar
steps on the stairs, then coming closer down the passage.
Already . . . As soon as this . . . Gun in hand, I heard the
knock, counted to five, called, 'Who is it?'

At the moment she entered the light came on. She stood
still, facing the barrel of my Luger. She didn't shout or
speak, just waited. Things had happened so fast my mind
needed time to catch up with them. For an instant I did

nothing, then fumbled my gun back inside my shirt.

We made jerky explanations. 'I didn't expect ... didn't recognise ...'

'The darkness ...'

6

WHAT have I done? Have I been mad? All evening the question has recurred to me, setting me shuddering. In the middle of one convulsion I stopped, detecting a strange rumble. My chair, pressed against a small table, had set this shuddering too.

It was Sunday, as it had to be, the only day I'm free in the evening now I work the first night shift.

'How about it then?' he'd said to me, near midnight of the day before. He was right behind me — normally I hear him come or feel him watching me. Not this time. I forced myself to look up at him. I realised again how tall he was, so that bent over my bench I was as much over-shadowed by him as I used to be by his namesake.

'Six o'clock, tomorrow?' He said. 'Ange Bleu?'

'Fine,' I said.

'See you,' he said.

I didn't tell Annya. It was something I had to face alone.

The evening church bells were ringing as I left my hotel. That's another thing I used not to understand; why these bells — which are used as an air-raid alarm in-stead of the despondent moaning sirens of other wars — never brought a raid or missile attack. Sunday is the day of the weekly test. Not just of the bells, of the action everyone should take in a real attack, but only a few old people turn out and the members of the Youth Leagues seem to make a point at these times of walking defiantly about the streets, their radios dangling from their wrists like ladies' handbags, giving them the life pulse they need. Most of the rest stay at home, as if they've grown bored or incredulous, and the authorities don't force them.

I try to see it as a good sign: they're defying their oppressors, refusing to conform. But it could also show how little danger there is now of air attack.

As I rounded the corner by the Ange Bleu a scurry of dead leaves came blowing past my feet and a gust of wind got inside my jacket. For the first time since spring I felt cold. I turned quickly through its door.

We sat in a dark alcove and at once, because he said little, I began to make conversation, as if to protect myself against what he might discover if we sat silent. Terrifyingly, I found myself talking about the number of machine failures there'd been recently at the factory — another four cutters and a lathe since those first three capstans. It had apparently been at the top of my mind, waiting for a chance to burst out. Unconsciously I had carried out that operation not to impress Annya, not as a hopeless signal to Ops, but as a signal to Harris. Was that your work? he'd say, his eyes opening wide so that for the first time I'd see into them. Well, well, well!

Instead he merely listened. I found his silence infuriating. 'Quite a coincidence, eh?' I went on. I was maddened by the way he seemed to be forcing me to elaborate. 'You any theories?'

Suddenly his silent refusal even to notice that I'd asked

him a question, gave me hope. Surely this *was* his answer. Wasn't he even growing impatient at my obtuseness? At that moment everything made a tidy pattern: the way he'd watched me all these months, chosen Annya for his secretary, forced this meeting on me. Although I knew it was all hypothesis, I didn't care. I discovered not merely a deep emotional desire to confide in him — which I already half knew about — but that the insane danger of this course was its attraction.

I confided in him.

So quickly that I was reacting to it before I understood it, he was holding out his hand to me beside but below the table. In a trance, back with that cold sprat, I took it — and did find something in it. A folded finger.

He *was* one of us. We went on sipping our watery beer, discussing the weather and the price of food, two work-mates out for a Sunday evening drink together. I did it as if in my sleep. I don't remember a single remark or idea. I could only sit there experiencing not so much happiness as a sense of ecstatic collapse. I was no longer alone. It was as if these past months I'd been supporting on my own a weight the vastness of which I only now understood.

More important — the implications spread — it meant we were still fighting. Each time that I'd disclosed myself to a new recruit — Lena, Annya — I'd half hoped to discover that they were already working for us and had retained the contact with Ops which I had lost. I'd felt a small disappointment that they were as alone as I was.

All the way home I moved in a haze of relief. I wanted to hum tunes. I fixed my face in a scowl in case my obvious happiness should make me conspicuous in this town of dismal people. It has taken several hours for my fear to reach its climax.

As I sit here waiting for Annya the wind is making a

strange whistling noise in some outside pipe. Probably it happened in summer too, but I didn't notice. The long sweltering days seemed still. Now in autumn I have begun to hear it, but till now I've been thinking it's the noise of a child playing a toy pipe in some house along the street. I've formed a clear picture of him there, piping in this mournful tuneless way.

'What's happened?' She guessed at once. I must have looked worse than I realised.

'Harris.'

'Go on.'

Her frightened stare made it hard for me to tell her. 'I've made contact.'

'With him!' She said it less with horror than with disbelief.

'Why not?'

She wouldn't answer, just stood staring, occasionally giving her head small shakes.

'He belongs. It's what we hoped.'

She stood at the window. She crossed towards the door, changed direction and sat on the bed. She seemed to feel caged. 'Why didn't you tell me?'

'I didn't know till the moment before I did it.' How unprofessional it sounded. 'Have you discovered something?'

No answer.

'If you have you must tell me.'

She went on sitting there, now looking down at the place on my pillow where Mr. Pete used to curl himself. I grew more confident that her alarm had been mere intuition.

'He gave me a sign,' I said, and described his handshake. She stared again. At last I seemed to have impressed her.

'We can easily check him. Family Choice.'

Annya took the message, not verbally — his room is probably bugged — but by note which she left in his in-tray. *'The White Cliffs of Dover.'*

For three anxious nights we've been listening. The jamming is now so bad the news bulletins are totally indecipherable and it needs concentration to make sense even of the entertainment programmes. It's not the crude high-pitched whines of a few months ago, but cleverly disguised as interference by local stations. Three are right on top of ours. One continuously broadcasts a time signal in the form of the opening notes of a well-known symphony; another reads gabbled Spanish news, female and male announcers alternating; a third seems all the time at the climax of some coloratura opera. Just when I particularly want to catch a request a soprano surges forwards, gripped by tragic and beautiful emotions which she's expressing at the very top of her range — perhaps because I would half like to listen I lose concentration.

Tonight it came. 'For Mum and Dad, from Irene, Bob, Carol, Whinney, Claude and little Cliff. To remind them of the old days: *The White Cliff's of Dover.*'

I clicked off the set.

I reached for Annya's hand. We looked into each other's eyes. Why do I remember this moment not as one of strength and hope but as one of more acute anxiety, greater loneliness, through which we reached towards each other more desperately?

7

I'm on my way to an early morning meeting with him. I've located his house — I could see it if I turned. In its suburban garden it might be anyone's. Inside I have no doubt he has a wife and children, dishwasher and cage of gerbils. I go no closer, but stand here facing this board fence, my collar turned up.

It's going to be one of those soft autumn days when the sun sometimes penetrates the mist around mid-morning but soon after lunch goes finally behind it. Such days are more to my taste than high summer. Though it's early, someone is already burning leaves. I can smell smoke.

Here in this quiet suburb I have again the feeling I used to get on my summer reconnaissances, that the world is growing still and I'm beginning to hear the faint rustle of things growing. Only this morning it's the sound of things gently closing, going down under.

Has he noticed me standing here, half hidden beside this board fence below a suburban ilex? I've long ago realised that if my worst fears are true, Family Choice could as easily be one of their fabrications as the rest of our broadcasts.

We sat in his study. Alone with him I felt, as I always do that he was playing with me. He seemed physically enormous. I had to struggle to remember his real size — big enough. I made myself stare him in the eyes, but then the parts of his mournful face which I wasn't staring at seemed grotesquely to elongate themselves till it had grown from its usual thirty centimetres to sixty.

But it was his mind that really seemed to engulf mine as I talked and talked about the low moral of this country and about the faith which keeps me fighting, and he listened and listened but didn't answer. That was his technique. It made me desperate. Continuously I seemed to reach a climax of uncertainty. It was as if I'd launched myself from some firm shore but had less and less idea whether I was going in a direction he approved. I'd begin to stumble over my words. I'd pass from anxiety to fury. I'd be about to yell at him to say *something*, just grunt if that was his thing. At this moment, as if he'd been profoundly attentive to all I'd been telling him, he'd say, 'I know just how you feel,' shaking his head with grave concern.

In the seconds which followed I'd feel shameless gratitude for his sympathy, withheld so long – and loathe myself for this feeling.

I told him about my visit with Lena to the Hospital for Social Diseases.

'You went there!'

'Right,' I said, swelling with horrible conceit at his admiration for my courage.

I mentioned my visit to the priest.

'What did you tell him?' He leant alertly forwards.

As if it had always been my intention, I said firmly, 'Not a thing.'

He relaxed. 'We've had trouble with him.'

I didn't mention my operation with Lena which failed.

All the time we talked I could hear a heavy whirring noise in some distant part of the house. His wife vacuum-cleaning? Just when I was convinced of this I'd seem to hear it as something quite soft but very close. A tape-recorder?

There's to be a circuit meeting. It seems that Detergent wasn't entirely extinguished. With infinite caution the remnants are being reassembled. They've known all along who I was supposed to be. They've been waiting till I convinced them I wasn't a plant.

Room 444B, Admin. Block at two p.m. I reserve final judgment, but already this meeting in the very heart of their organisation rings true.

Annya is to come. In each other's presence we shall be better able to judge him. We shall be able to look away from him and shame each other out of our trapped-animal states of mind.

At one fifty-five I came through the subterranean passage and rode the lift to the fourth floor. How simple it seemed. All I'd needed was a pass he'd given me for a visit to the labour counsellor. It's in his office we're meeting.

He's a new appointment, I was told, part doctor, part analyst, part staff officer. Commissar might be the old-fashioned word.

In theory he's there to direct people to the jobs which suit their skills and emotions, but in practice he's a further sieve for eliminating troublemakers and security risks without the sackings and redundancies which once caused strikes. Now people are told they'd be well advised to visit their doctor.

He's part of our circuit, Harris says: Aerial. The most valuable person we could have. Even top executives are scared of him in case he reports them as emotional security risks. Provided he's on our side, every resistance worker in the factory is safe.

He had bushy white hair and a little white goatee

beard — as soon as I saw him I realised that his job had made me expect some such histrionic appearance. He rose from his desk, took my hand in a gentle grip and used it to direct me to a chair. No cold sprat this time.

All the others it seemed were here before me. Harris to my right, Annya to my left, both slightly behind me. Beyond Aerial's desk a young man with a dark beard sat near the window as if keeping watch out of it, one hand held inside his jacket where it could quickly reach a shoulder holster. I gave no sign of recognition, even to Annya. This whole long summer has taught me that today we must keep to our parts in all but the most exceptional circumstances.

So when Aerial began to ask me if I was happy in my work, and what I thought of the new piece-rate incentive scheme I gave him straight, nervous-employee answers. Suddenly — as if there'd been some signal I'd missed — he said without change of tone, 'Okay, Ajax, well done.'

At once everyone was relaxing in their chairs and smiling. It was as if I'd passed some test and my examiners, normal people again, were congratulating me.

The real business began. Disconcertingly, I found that they knew less than I did. True, they had kept radio contact with Ops, but they seemed to believe that I, as newest arrival, could expand and give humanity to the bare instructions they received. What sort of person was Judd? Aerial asked. Apparently he'd never met him.

They were childishly anxious for news of the Second Coming. I hinted. I'd have invented if I hadn't feared I'd be proved wrong, or say something they knew to be false.

Still more surprising, they seemed to have made little progress towards guessing the true function of this factory they have infiltrated. The Admin. Block is even more rigidly divided into two than I'd guessed: they all work on the side concerned with the factory itself, which provides a second bluff façade.

As with Harris, I talked too much, but they encouraged me, especially Aerial. He watched me more than he watched Harris, as if he thought my advice might be better. I was flattered.

'So what should we do?' he asked.

I said we could only ask Ops for instructions — destroy at once or plan for the big night? — when we could tell them whether it was military headquarters, decoding station, centre for propaganda, or whatever else we discovered it to be. Even at this moment, excited by their attention, something made me avoid coming closer to my real guess. It was too vague. I was too unsure.

It followed that our first priority was to discover what we faced, I continued, and modestly suggested that night work was my speciality. They agreed. We discussed entrances, locks, sentries and dates.

We shook hands. Aerial produced a bottle of black-market whisky. I found those final minutes most disturbing. These people who I wanted to trust were taking a small but unnecessary risk. I didn't want their whisky, still less their chat which now became violent and bitter in its criticism of the regime.

The meeting over, Harris signalled to me with his eyes to stay. As we stood watching Annya and Daz — the bearded boy by the window — go out I saw his eyes follow Daz. Their look of concern, even fondness, but exasperation told me exactly what he felt: that Daz's boastful enthusiasm was a danger to us. Harris had nothing special to say to me. I believe he kept me because he'd noticed my distress. I believe he gave Daz that anxious look to reassure *me*.

By the time I reached the passage Annya was no longer in sight. I had no time to look for her: my shift began in seven minutes. Anyway I would see her later. Soon after midnight when I came home exhausted and dizzied by eight hours of howling machines I was so sure I'd find her waiting for me that I could only stand in my doorway staring with disbelief into my empty room.

Had she been arrested? Was she even now being fed truth drugs, or if they thought her useless having her brain injected to reduce it to a sponge for ever? Worse, was she *enjoying* some new sadistic rite they were performing on her, looking back on our love as something lukewarm and pathetic.

Pacing below the tent-ceiling on my pale green room three steps each way, I found myself cursing her for making me so anxious. 'Shit, shit, Christ shit on her . . .' Suddenly what I was doing seemed familiar. Jane and Hubby. A day when I'd suspected they were reconciled and laughing together at the pathetic lover I'd been, when I'd walked by the winter river, cursing her . . . For weeks I should have known it. I didn't merely love Annya. I was in love with her.

It's the most dangerous development yet. As if Judd's warning hadn't been enough . . . as if real love wasn't twice as dangerous as popsy love . . . as if I could forget where it had already led me . . .

I didn't care, that was the worst of it. When I was a child I had the falling dreams most children have. I was dropping, dropping. I believe my school friends when they told me that if I ever reached bottom I would die. For some years now I've stopped being frightened by these falling dreams. I still get them and for a few seconds I feel the old terror, then I pass through it and let myself fall. This dropping, or dying — the two remain linked in my mind — is a pleasure. That's what my falling in love with Annya is like. It terrifies me and I know I should struggle against it — but I won't.

I love the way she touches things, the clumsy way she squats on the floor, her heels beside her wide buttocks. I love her freckles which are so thick and dark on her shoulders they merge, but which thin so quickly on her back and chest. Because of her freckles her skin looks as if it should be rough but it's smoother than any I ever touched. Even those thin white scars — with my eyes shut I can scarcely detect them. About the movements or features of other women, the way they curl their little fingers or bend their hands back at the wrist, my first feeling is often revulsion. Even for ones I've loved I've had these instants of disgust before love has arrived, love for exactly these slightly repulsive gestures. With Annya there's no interval. Everything she is and does I love at once.

My love for Jane was childish. We had fun. My love for Lena was adolescent. We believed we could help each other. My love for Annya is based on the fact that we know that ultimately we can't help each other. As we cling together we each see these two lonely people, holding on to each other, believing nothing, achieving nothing except perhaps a tiny fragment of dignity in their own tiny self-estimations by admitting their own futility.

Last night as I waited for her, thinking these things, she was in my doorway before I heard her steps.

She stood looking in at me. Before either of us spoke, an important and identical revelation seemed to come to us. It was as if our minds together tracked back ten hours to room 444B, office of the labour counsellor, rendezvous for revived Detergent — and believed none of it.

Supporting evidence came later as we analysed our disbelief. Daz, sitting in that phoney sentry's position at the window, hand inside his jacket: if we were to be disturbed it wouldn't be through a fourth-floor window. Aerial paying me such exaggerated attention. Most suspicious, their apparent lack of knowledge about the concealed side of the Admin. Block.

Why then this elaborate charade? That wasn't difficult. To use me to feed back false information. To discover through me how much Ops knows — I suppressed a glow of self-approval at the way I'd kept my best guess to myself.

We made fresh plans. While pretending to work with them we must continue to investigate privately, but because any day they might reverse their policy our time was no longer unlimited.

There's a second doorway at the rear of Harris's office which she says he sometimes goes through, unlocking it first and relocking it behind him. It wasn't mentioned when our circuit studied plans and discussed routes. Theoretically it leads only to a store. It seems a good place to start.

Our problem may be its lock. From her description it sounds suspiciously like a safety model which I might not manage. He keeps his key in his pocket. Our eyes meeting, I asked her whether this was something she could handle. She said no word but her steady stare gave me her answer.

8

BUT she must not come here to tell me whether she has succeeded. We must never again meet in my room. Though we had talked in whispers, running my electric razor for extra cover, this procedure was itself suspicious. Parting, we agreed that we must meet outside at a pre-arranged rendezvous, and that to fix this we would use a dead-letter box behind the first of some metal railings in the street which leads to the factory gate.

I would leave a message there late on Friday as I left work and she would collect it when she went to work on Saturday morning. It would name a place and a time for Sunday, the only day when we were both free before midnight. As an extra precaution the time I would give in my message would be two hours after the actual time, and the café I would name would be two before the actual café in a list of five which we memorised.

To add to our difficulties, since the afternoon's meeting we both suspected we were being tailed. If, at the time of the rendezvous, either of us knew it was still happening, she would wear her coat buttoned instead of open, and I would carry my newspaper in my pocket instead of my hand. We would pass each other and move the hour one forward and the rendezvous one down the list.

This morning she was already sitting at the Café du Paye, but her black plastic coat was buttoned. It was five days since I'd seen her. I'd suffered greater loneliness than I'd expected. The extra hour I now had to wait seemed scarcely bearable. I longed to be careless and take the risk

of sitting there. To be so near her and have to pass by . . .
As acutely as my own distress I felt hers, sitting there in
that cheap black coat, a coffee in front of her which she
hadn't tasted, staring at the pavement.

At twelve I was first at the Bistro, my newspaper still in
my hand. I was about to sit when I saw her black coat
coming towards me, again buttoned. I began to curse her
for her failure to give her tail the slip. To control myself I
did sit. She passed within a yard of my chair without one
glance. Her tail must have passed soon after but I failed to
pick him.

We'd arranged to move the hour and place forward in
steps which increased in geometric series: one, two, four,
eight . . . At ten minutes to two I reached the Bon Jour
Bar. Too long to sit waiting in my nervous state. I passed
it, planning to turn in a few hundred metres and come
back. As soon as I turned I saw him: my own tail.

Caught too close to me, he'd pretended a sudden urge
to stare into a shop window — of women's bras. He was
one of the worst tails I've known. There he stood, not even
able to stop himself giving me glances out of the corner of
his eye. Returning past him, newspaper pocketed, I was
tempted to say a polite good morning. I'd only gone ten
steps further when I saw Annya coming towards me. For
the third time her black shiny coat was buttoned.

As soon as she'd passed I also stopped and stared into a
shop window. Things had gone too far — I must find
another way. Deciding that I would follow her, about
to start, I suddenly remembered *her* tail. Lucky I did
because at that exact moment he came past, less of an
amateur than mine, but still easy to pick this time in his
belted mackintosh and slouch hat.

I was again about to start when it happened a second
time: another, like the first but in Tyrolean hat with

feather. Either my first guess had been wrong or that tail himself had a tail.

I left a longer pause then set off after this one, repassing my own who was still window-shopping. Glancing back and seeing him now in clumsy pursuit, I suddenly pictured the procession the five of us were making. Though I suspected that there was some way to turn this to our advantage, I couldn't yet think how.

When we'd proceeded like this for several streets, at the end of a straight stretch which had forced my man to keep unusually far behind, I turned ostentatiously out of sight down a side road and at once stepped into the entrance of a bank. Here I reversed my coat, brown lining outwards, put on the hat and glasses I'd brought in its pocket, hid my newspaper and slipped the limping wedge I've made for such emergencies into the heel of my left shoe. I returned round the corner the moment before I calculated he would arrive there. It worked perfectly. He came hurrying past me without a glance and turned out of sight where I'd turned. Now I was able to recross the end of that side road, going in my original direction, before he would have fully registered that he'd lost me. I covered thirty metres at a brisk lope before slowing to a hobble.

Despite the delay I should by now have been close to Annya and her tails, but I couldn't find them. I peered back in case I'd over run them. I hurried forward again.

I became less hopeful. By now I'd passed many turns down which she might have led them. Suddenly, only ten paces ahead, the one in the Tyrolean hat with feather was coming *towards* me. I was so surprised I only just prevented myself halting to stare at him. Had he left the pursuit? Had Annya turned back so that she was now behind me? To follow him would take me back along the route which my own tail must now be checking.

I had four hours to fill till our next rendezvous at six at L'Americano. One hour had made me desperate. A period four times as long. I went to a cinema and watched a war propaganda film. It ended in trumpets and glory. It began again and reached the point at which I'd entered. I still forced myself to stay. It was already five when I had a maddening doubt. Had Annya understood my whispered instructions about a geometric series, or had she for example thought I merely meant arithmetical increases of one, two, three, four hours? If so, had she come to Le Bistro at five?

I hurried from the cinema. Panting heavily I arrived there, but it was now five-ten and there was no sign of her. At six I waited at L'Americano. She didn't come. I hardly expected her. As that last fifty minutes had passed I'd grown more certain that I'd missed her at five at Le Bistro. If so I must now go at nine to the Café du Paye. Alternatively, on my geometric reckoning, I had eight hours to wait till two in the morning at the Grand Prix.

Quite soon I knew I should never keep that next rendezvous. She was avoiding me. These last five days she'd been interfered with. All the resistance and anger I'd rebuilt in her had been broken down. I'd been idiotic to leave her alone so long. Even if these were false fears, as I prayed they were, she'd think I'd failed her at five and would now guess she'd misunderstood our arrangement. I'd no idea how she might try to put herself right — or too many ideas.

As soon as I knew I was going to abandon my sensible plans for our rendezvous and do something far more dangerous I ceased to be nervous. I also ceased to find waiting so unbearable. It had been dark for several hours when I came to the address.

By a coincidence which had shocked me when she first told me it was in Avenue Georges, that street from which number 125 was missing, though at the opposite end. I rang the brass bell beside the heavy painted door. No one answered. I pushed it open and came into a hall lit only by light from an open doorway. Inside this an old woman sat in a chair with a blanket over her knees.

She seemed to be doing nothing except watch the door and wait for arrivals. Something clicked in my memory. As soon as I gave her Annya's name, without moving her hands from below the blanket, she said a room number.

I climbed stairs and went along a passage lit by a shade-less bulb hanging on a wire, still hunting in my mind for the association. As I passed one of the numbered doors I heard from behind it the sound of low male words. Instantly that distinctive murmur created the scene beyond the door and I knew the business of that old woman, and the function of Annya's lodging house.

She let me in and locked the door. She had no choice, but she was terrified. Unable to speak, she could only stand with her back to the closed door and stare at me. She was frightened by my loss of self-control in coming here — by my hat and dark glasses, too, perhaps — but her staring silence told me she had another cause for alarm. *Her* room was bugged. Instantly I knew the only way to protect her. I must be a customer. Nothing else would explain to the listening bug my late-night call.

The idea seemed to occur to us at the same moment.

'Hallo, love.'

'Hallo, dearie.' We spoke almost together.

It was a weird love-making. At first, no doubt because of her sense that we were performing to an audience, she was untypically stiff and reluctant. She tried to fight me off. She bit my shoulder so violently that I could feel warm blood. I was unlike myself too, bitterly suspicious that all the time I'd known her she had been living in this brothel, having visitors of the sort I was now acting. I was rough, even vicious, enjoying forcing her to admit me as client not lover. I tore at her clothes. I threw her down. Before she could recover I was trying to take her where she'd fallen, her body and buttocks on the bed, her legs and feet hanging to the floor. At the same time I kept making in-character remarks. 'Here, what's all the fuss? This the way you usually carry on? Anyone'd think you weren't happy in your work.'

Her terror seemed to increase, as if she was unsure whether I was acting or in earnest. Perhaps I too became uncertain. When at last I entered her she gave such a scream I thought I'd injured her.

After that things changed. Lying beside me in the darkness, she cried, not violently as she sometimes does but quietly, to herself, as if she'd retreated to some place where I could no longer reach her.

I called her darling. I never have before. I held her tightly.

'It's no use,' she said.

'Of course it is,' I whispered. Was she telling me that in these last five days she'd been broken? Or did it refer to her attempts to find a way past that locked door?

'We can't give up,' I whispered, confident that the bug would take this to refer to some such problem as boozer's prick or premature ejaculation.

'I tried,' she said. 'I really tried.'

'There's a way. There must be.'

Presently she was holding me in her arms. 'Oh Alec.' It was how she often held me after love. Once again I was disturbed by this sudden reversal of our roles, from my pitying her to her pitying me. I was even more worried by the rash way she'd used my name openly.

Putting my mouth close to her ear, lower than any bug could detect, I whispered, 'The key?' She lay quite still. Had I said it too quietly? I said it again. At once, as if she'd heard the first time, I felt her give a quick nod in the darkness.

Part Three

I

TOMORROW I shall go.

It's three days now since I should have set out for the frontier, but I've stayed hiding here in this town, making excuses.

I've changed rooms twice more, once the night it happened, once tonight. That first night I lowered both my suitcases into the canal, filled with all my equipment except the small bag of rations I've been collecting. My Luger went too, but not its shoulder holster. Into this I fitted that small reel of tape.

Alone it keeps me going. The whole purpose of my existence seems centred in this small hard package under my left arm which I must carry home and deliver.

All day I stay in these new mean rooms — I can no longer work at the factory, of course — listening for howling sirens, slamming car doors, heavy feet on the stairs.

I'm in continual fear, but I stay because to go terrifies me more.

Incredible how attractive my life here — even the few fragments of it I can still experience — has become. Till now I've assumed it was a nightmare from which I was longing to escape. As for the nostalgia I feel for earlier times, not merely for my relationships with Lena and Annya, but for my evenings with the Patrases, my work at the factory, my walks to work on summer mornings when I was still on day shift, my sleepless nights all those hot months when the town lay silent except for the screams of the Youth League, even for far smaller things, the coarse feel of utility sheets, the taste of substitute instant coffee, the sight of ill-dressed children playing in the streets — this especially . . .

My reluctance is like the reluctance I used to feel at work to press the red button which brought my shuddering machine and my machine-like hands to rest for the day and meant I must return to a real world of choice and action. Or on those summer nights of reconnaissance, which I'd spend in a ditch beside one of the arterial roads, wrapped in my plastic cape, a cocoon-like ball which the dew would run down in rivulets but inside which I'd be dry and warm, when with the greatest reluctance, the first light of dawn growing clearer every moment in the north-eastern sky, I'd break myself out of this cocoon to hurry home before the Patrases woke.

Is it because I can look ahead and picture more clearly my arrival? So this happened, I shall tell them in the dry factual way which is our tradition, followed by this and presently by this. As a result I bring them this. With a culminating act of modesty I shall toss it on to Judd's desk and my work will be done. But it won't be an act because at that moment I shall suffer total indifference. Not the smallest part of me will care whether or not Judd's grey-whiskered face creases into approval — if it ever could. Finally I shall understand that I am my own judge and — here's the rub — I shan't care about my verdict.

Or is it because I still can't accept the fact the Annya has gone first? As I hurry furtively along dark streets at night, making brief foolish sorties, trying to trick myself into an impulsive departure, I find myself visiting again and again those five cafés we listed, as if I only hope that by reliving that day I shall get some message she left for me but I never understood. Once I even went to our dead-letter box and felt behind the railings in case somewhere among the drift of autumn leaves I'd missed a letter which would explain.

I turned back in alarm at what I was doing and hurried home. But part of my mind still refuses to accept the word never. Surely somewhere, sometime in some form I haven't yet imagined there will be a message.

We met at one a.m., in an angle of the outer wall of the factory. The night was black, the waning moon still many hours away even if it would ever penetrate the cold rain-filled mist which was rolling in dense drifts across the concrete yard. It was so dark that we lost each other if we got more than three paces apart, and to prevent this I held her hand as I led her along the brickwork towards the pipe we'd chosen. Twenty metres above us in the night it passed the window she'd left unlatched — side window to Harris's office.

Even on a warm day, even with the cords I'd prepared, a twenty-metre climb up a drain pipe would have been a test. That night the moisture on the icy painted metal made it so slippery I stood for several seconds staring up into the blackness, wondering whether there was some alternative.

I went ahead. I must be first to attempt that final sideways scramble to the window ledge across a metre of bare wall. I would have preferred to be below her. She came up with terrible slowness. Continually I had to whisper encouragements down to her. 'Nearly there now.' I was afraid that in her alarm she'd forget to keep her cord round the pipe, or that she'd slip at the moment she had to untie it to pass one of the wall fixings. Quite soon I knew from the way she wasn't answering that her mouth was set in something close to panic. Presently I could hear small whimpering sounds. She was crying with fear. But she still climbed. If I'd been as unathletic and as terrified, would I have shown such courage?

A new surge of wet mist hid the ground from us. We climbed in an isolated world of our own, coated in cold and clammy air, which without actually falling like rain settled on all parts of us and ran down our necks and into our eyes.

Reaching far to my left, I picked at the metal window with my finger-nails, separated it from the frame and pulled it open. The bottom of the metal frame was only two or three centimetres deep. Hooking the top joints of the fingers of my left hand over this, I untied my cord with my right hand, grabbed for the frame with this hand too and let myself fall free. My grip held, but for several seconds I hung at arm's length, wondering if I'd have the strength to haul myself up. I imagined myself dangling pathetically there till my fingers finally grew too weak. Would I last one minute or fifteen? With a jerk I did it and tumbled head and shoulders downwards into the black office.

'First untie your cord.' Leaning from the window I spoke with sternness, almost anger, to her dark shape which I could see protruding from the surface of the wall. She made no sound.

'Annya, can you hear? Annya, if you can hear me . . .'

A tiny dried-up croak, like the first cracking apart of surfaces adhered together with phlegm.

'Hold on to the pipe with your right hand. Whatever you do, don't let go. Now reach to the left with your left.' Slowly I talked her in. 'No, not my wrist, my hand. Hold my hand.'

Presently she was hanging below me, a huge limp weight. 'When I say climb, use your feet against the wall.'

But she just hung. Her silence gave me a strange direct message to stop attempting something impossible, something which because it was impossible had become somehow improper. Even when she was lying sacklike, half across the sill, I had to take handfuls of her slacks and sweater to lift her in.

We sat on the floor, pulling socks over our shoes. We felt our way along the walls to that rear door. All the way I obscurely sensed Harris's presence. In spite of the fact that we were making our reconnaissance two days before our circuit had arranged it, I'd half expected to find him sitting in the darkness waiting for us. The key I'd cut from the soap impression she'd taken worked stiffly. We passed through the door and closed it softly.

Dark as it had been in his office, we were now in a more intense and total blackness. As I moved cautiously forward I had to control a continuous desire to hold up my forearm to protect my face. Annya came close behind. I'd only gone a few paces when I stumbled down several steps and landed heavily on my knees.

At once I began to reach back for her, moving my hands right and left. When, after several empty sweeps, I touched her leg I had the strange impression that she hadn't been feeling for me but waiting to see if I found her.

Now she went ahead, her night sight better than mine, leading me by the wrist. Increasingly I sensed that she knew where she was going. Beyond the penetrating of that door I'd made no plan.

We turned several times. Though I counted our paces in each new direction the route became dangerously complicated. 'You know the way back?' Perhaps she didn't hear. She pulled me faster.

We seemed to reach a wide hall. The walls fell away and the small rustles of our sock-covered shoes now went up to a remote ceiling. Presently I could make out, close ahead, something which looked like a vast molehill. It was unlit except at its top where I thought I detected a very faint glow, just enough to give the slightest luminosity to the air immediately above. A soundless by heavy vibration which was shaking this whole hall seemed to come from that great molehill's centre.

'Wait here.'

She left me. Minute after minute I crouched in the darkness. I'd have felt more secure if I'd been against a wall instead of in the open with nothing I could feel or see except this vast black shape ahead of me. Though I sometimes thought that it was so close I could put out a hand and touch it, at other times I believed it was several metres away. I began to imagine the rustle of sock-covered shoes all around me. I turned sharply, sure that someone was so close I'd felt their breath. At the same moment, clear and unmistakable in this blackness which concentrated all my senses in my ears, I heard the distant thud of a door. Somewhere below us in this building someone else was active.

At once, but so remote that for a second it didn't seem

to concern me, I heard loud whistles being blown outside in the night. For the briefest instant I suspect that Annya had betrayed me, then she was close again.

'What happened?'

'I got it.'

Was it that moment when I'd doubted her which made me refuse to go the way she began to pull me but instead set off pulling her back the way we'd come? Would things otherwise have ended differently? Now I occasionally flashed my torch as we ran, hunting for a staircase. I found one. We were five steps down when, only a floor below, a shocking clatter and scraping began, as if someone was forcing an entrance through an unused door. An instant later metal-studded boots came running with ringing slams along a concrete passage towards us. We turned and fled upwards.

They followed us up. 'Run to the top,' I told her. I stood at a bend, Luger in my right hand, torch at arm's length in my left. For a second I shone it. Instantly I saw flashes below me — I have no memory of the noise the shots must have made. I fired three times towards the flashes. There was a yell, more of fury than pain and the sound of something soft falling down several stairs. I turned and ran on up. Three floors above at the top of a narrow flight without a rail I reached a hatchway. Twice more I fired into the darkness below though I could hear no pursuit, then went through the hatch closing it behind me.

I was on the building's roof. Things were different: the night was no longer black but startlingly bright. Though the wet mist was still around, everywhere it had been driven back or transformed into white smoky wisps. For an instant I didn't understand why, then I saw the searchlight, halfway up a facing building, shining directly on to our roof. I think Annya was dazed too because she was standing fully in its beam — perhaps they'd just switched on. I pulled her below the parapet.

I found a bolt on the hatch and pushed it across. The slamming of that bolt ended the second-by-second reactions which had carried me from the hall of the molehill up to this roof. Looking around for our next move, seeing the roof rising at forty-five degrees behind us every metre of its grey slate lit by that searchlight, my mind seemed to change from the fastest possible activity to none at all. We hadn't escaped. We'd trapped ourselves.

I became so mentally numb I couldn't understand why Annya was showing me a small spool of tape. What did it mean? I was further confused by a voice shouting through a megaphone from below. The words seemed senseless, though the voice was familiar.

'Alec Meyer, you've done well.' Harris.

'That's where we want her.' How could he possibly be complimenting me?

'Meyer, if you harm her . . .' Now he seemed to threaten. It was as if he needed badly to persuade me to do something and in his anxiety was using tactic after tactic in unconvincing haste. Suddenly I understood: her tape. It was our success. It held the secret of this building.

Half kneeling half lying together against the slates below that low parapet, she was trying to give it to me, but when I took hold of it she didn't let go. Believing I'd misunderstood her, I also let go, but at once she pushed it towards me again. Now I guessed. I was to take it home. She was handing me the journey I must make, with all its danger and near certainty of death. Of course she was reluctant.

It meant more. Always till now we'd pretended that the

life of secrecy and fear we were living together was temporary. Somewhere ahead was a time when we would be together and free. Without a word we both now gave up that belief. Nothing had changed. The chance that we would both escape had always been small — it had got no smaller. We had merely ceased to believe in it. With certainty we saw that it had always been a pretence.

This is the moment I remember. The moment when we lost each other, when a duty to something beyond herself — perhaps to me — made her push me away. Because I understood how doing it was destroying her, because I realised with a certainty I'd never felt before that I *had* possessed her, all of her, I accepted the loneliness and separation she was giving me.

Regret, rebellion against something so unnecessary, followed quickly.

'We'll go together.'

She didn't answer.

'Come on.' I began to look left and right along the bright roof but didn't move. She hardly seemed to hear. Increasingly she seemed to listen to that voice which had never ceased to call to us from below.

'Mayer, I'm appealing to you.'

The things I was saying seemed a distraction which almost annoyed her. I began to guess that part of the purpose of these shouts might be to divide us — though they had a more obvious function: to explain to the crowd gathered down there what was happening. 'Gunman holds girl hostage.' A neat cliché-slot in their minds was being filled, to be convincingly confirmed by tomorrow's papers.

'Mayer, if you have conditions, please stand and call them out clearly.'

She grew more disturbed. 'What shall I do?' She spoke more to herself than to me.

'What can either of us do?' I corrected her.

She kept silent, as if realising that nothing could unsay her slip.

I stopped hunting for ingenious escape plans — there weren't any. I told her we must crawl in opposite directions below the parapet. After about ten metres she must momentarily show herself, so creating a diversion which could give me a slim extra chance. I took the tape from her.

She turned and began to crawl. She turned back. There seemed something she'd forgotten to say. Or was her courage failing? Had she all the time been hoping that I'd tell her we needn't part? 'What are you waiting for?' I yelled at her.

I'd gone about six metres when I looked back, intending to watch for the moment when she showed herself. Amazed, I saw that instead of allowing an arm or buttock to appear momentarily above the parapet, giving the impression of an accidental exposure and suggesting we were both moving in that direction, she was getting to her feet. A second later she was in full view.

I stood too, and ran towards her. I ran in tense terror, expecting at any second to hear the first crackle of explosions from below as they began to shoot or see her drop to her knees as she was hit. I must force her to crouch with me and invent a new plan, now she'd spoiled this one. Halfway, I saw her glance back, see me and start to run herself.

She was running to Harris, that was what she wanted me to think. It was her last and bravest attempt to drive me to my duty.

I came close behind her. She turned to face me. I had to

tell her that I understood what she was doing and why. I put out my hands to grip her wrists. Search in my memory as I will I find no other thought than this, followed instantly by that final horror as she tried to step away from me, caught the back of her calves against the parapet and sat into space.

I remember her scream, wild and loud as she understood what had happened, cut to half volume as she passed below the parapet. That wasn't the end. She screamed all the way down. I couldn't look. I sank to my knees. I crossed my arms on my chest and lowered my head. I shut my eyes and tried to shut my ears. Clearly I could imagine her. Her legs and arms weren't fighting the air but her back was twisting and writhing — just as I'd imagined Mr. Pete's.

My love for her, reaching climax at that moment, seems to coexist with this rather unattractive final picture of her.

2

THERE are voices out there. Several men's I don't know, and one woman's I seem to recognise.

I have been hidden below this floor for forty-eight hours. My supplies are running low. I must come out before my strength goes — or the smell of my excrement gives me away.

Making water is easy — though I have to be careful it doesn't hiss and bubble. Moving my bowels while lying on my side is harder — especially since I'm taking no exercise, eating no roughage and therefore growing constipated. This morning — I think it was morning — I managed to expel several bullet-hard goat's pellets. I heard them rattle as they tumbled sideways across my lower buttock on to the boards.

Incredible luck. I have joined an escape line. I'm handed from person to person, always at night. By day I wait in thickets or if I'm lucky in roadmenders' huts. My helpers never show their faces but keep them turned away in the shadows of their cars. Some wear scarves wound across their mouths and noses.

I had been going south, travelling by the sun, keeping a rough check on my progress towards the frontier by guessing my walking speed. Now I've lost all count. It's possible they may be taking me in some quite different direction, towards some other destination. I can only hope and trust. Besides, why should they take such trouble with me? . . .

Near the end of my endurance, I risked hitching a lift. I was so hungry and such a bitter wind was blowing from the centre of the continent that I believe otherwise I'd never have seen sunrise but been found like some tramp, a frosty heap in the morning. My summer clothes and coat are hopelessly thin.

He braked and stopped beyond me. Slowly I walked towards his red lights, controlling a strong urge to plunge into the roadside undergrowth.

He was alone. He was young. After only ten minutes I knew I must trust him . . .

Their method is to drop me after the night's ride, often lasting no more than half an hour, and tell me what time next evening to emerge and wait for the next.

No one stopped. I'm alone again. I didn't dare linger by the road, giving that almost imperceptible sign as the lights of car after car dazzled me, when any one of them might have been crammed with police — if as I feared my escape line had been blown.

I doubt whether it matters. The frontier is nearer, perhaps very near indeed. I know because the country has changed and I'm already in foothills. Ahead in the day-time I sometimes see high up the sky a line of snowy peaks.

The air is thinner. Small exertions make me pant for breath. The nights are even more bitterly cold.

My mind is affected too. I seem increasingly to move in a dreamlike condition. I find myself crouching minutes at a time, convinced that twenty metres ahead I saw something dodge behind a rock.

Every day I move further forward into this high land. It's clean up here. The air is clear. It's getting very quiet.

Despite my fears, in fact I see fewer and fewer people, at most one or two each day and these usually on distant mountain paths at the far sides of valleys. They, too, seem to be alone and going at a slow pace, much like mine, in the same direction. Will a whole group of us meet at the frontier? More likely we shall go on separately each to our own private stretch of barbed wire, mines and machine-guns.

Today I saw one hurrying in the opposite direction. I found the clumsy way he hurried, sometimes stumbling and even falling, very disturbing. Was he running in terror from something ahead?

I see houses too, but because I keep to the ridges and never descend into the valleys I don't pass close to them. Mostly they are of farm-chalet style, and this is no doubt why they seem both strange and familiar. Strange because I've never till now visited mountain country, but familiar from childhood storybooks. It may account for the sadness they give me. Suddenly I see one standing quite still in a crease of a hill. It's lit by mountain sunshine. Up here on its sloping pastures, it seems to say that life is short, even its life, and the struggle to be different from nature can't last more than a short time. Already I seem to see its granite walls a few years from now when the winter gales have torn off its roof and blown out its doors and windows. These mountain houses are quite unlike the smug houses built on plains, which exude a small-minded confidence that they'll stand for ever.

Though the houses themselves have personality, I have never seen any farmers or peasants near them. They might already be deserted. Some I think are.

Harris was cross-examining me. I'd been captured. I'd been tortured. They'd set my feet in dry-ice so that I could no longer feel them. Now they were bringing hammers with which to crack the bones — odd how my unconscious mind reverted to these earlier practices, forgetting what I now know. Harris's role was the familiar one. Physically broken but heroically silent, I'd been brought to him. I was defiant. I'd rather die than speak. I saw him with loathing, tried to spit at him — and he was kind to me.

The first kindness I'd received for twenty-one days — I knew the exact period. He made them sit me in a chair, offered me a cigarette. He didn't need to speak. My mind leapt to the conclusion which these two gestures implied. I longed to confess to him, could hardly wait to tell him everything I knew. The part of myself which still resisted, I hated.

'We rather admire you,' he began.

I felt nothing for him but love.

'You've done pretty well. Incidentally' — a small un-happy laugh — 'you've eliminated two of our best agents. But I hardly need to tell you that . . .'

Silently I implied that he was right, that all along I'd known who they were, used them till they were of no value to me, then destroyed them. He could never know that Annya had slipped.

'You realise, of course, that your tape is a plant. It carries information designed to deceive your employ-ers.'

Could it be true? I felt appalling fear. So after all I had failed.

But if it was true surely he wouldn't have told me. He was lying. He couldn't accept the fact that Annya *had* loved me. I smiled at him. I felt no anger. My victory was complete.

He smiled back, accepting it. I'd forced him to.

'You thought we were testing you too hard.' At about this point he ceased to be Harris and became Colonel Judd. I saw that long face with those unmilitary grey side-whiskers. '. . . Resented the way we left you . . . Work out your own salvation . . .' Even his speech took on the tongue-tied, cliché-struck quality of that uniformed dummy whose mind had congealed for ever when he was given charge of a clandestine warfare unit. But he, too, in his inarticulate way, was trying to forgive and con-gratulate me.

My dream ended before I had a chance to confess to them. It didn't matter, because I would have done. I woke in a state of amazing happiness. I was permeated by a kind of bliss — I know no other word. I longed to return to this dream.

Opening my eyes, I saw that all parts of my clothes

from my coat to my exposed feet were covered in white frost. In the last few seconds the sun had reached them, making them shine and glitter. Already I seemed to feel its warmth.

I'm near the end.

All day I've climbed through grey cloud which sweeps over these hills, hiding every rock or bush beyond five paces.

For an instant it clears showing me a glimpse of grey sky, a mountain peak where I didn't expect one, then I'm lost again in a thick icy blanket. My clothes are so wet I could wring cupfuls of water from them, if the thought of touching them with my sodden fishmonger's hands didn't make me shiver more heavily.

Now in the evening I'm clear of the cloud and ahead of me there's a bare upland plateau. It's the bleakest place I've ever seen. The grass is brown, not from sun but from the bitter wind which moans across it all year.

Somewhere out there — it may not even be marked — is the frontier.

Now the terrible reluctance which has grown in me every day of my journey is unbearable. It makes me want to cry like a child — if there was anyone here to cry to.

I realise more clearly the reason for my terror. It's not that I'm afraid to cross in case I discover that my country no longer exists and I'm thus condemned to remain for ever in some neutral internment camp. It's because I'm afraid it may exist, but has some idiotic bureaucratic regulation which forbids it ever to send me back.

Because to succeed I've needed to become the person I am, a person totally unfitted for the country I once knew, fit only for this life of struggle and fear, love and destruction.

Tonight, when the moon sets, I shall go forward towards the barbed-wire and machine-guns, knowing that at the last I shan't even hear the burst which kills me, carrying with me this conviction — and my tape. In my mind the two grow alike.

ALSO AVAILABLE IN CORONET BOOKS

THOMAS HINDE

☐ 18298 9   The Day The Call Came   35p
☐ 19491 X   Generally a Virgin   40p

PETER FEIBLEMAN

☐ 19895 8   The Columbus Tree   80p

GEORGE FEIFER

☐ 18778 6   The Girl From Petrovka   40p

JOSEPH HONE

☐ 19490 1   Private Sector   50p

THOMAS TRYON

☐ 18811 1   Harvest Home   60p

CYNTHIA BUCHANAN

☐ 18065 X   Maiden   40p

All these books are available at your local bookshop or newsagent, or can be ordered direct from the publisher. Just tick the titles you want and fill in the form below.

....

CORONET BOOKS, P.O. Box 11, Falmouth, Cornwall.

Please send cheque or postal order, and allow the following for postage and packing:

UK AND EIRE – 15p for the first book plus 5p per copy for each additional book ordered to a maximum charge of 50p.
OVERSEAS CUSTOMERS AND B.F.P.O. – please allow 20p for the first book and 10p per copy for each additional book.

Name ....

Address ....

....